FROM MEN TO MONSTERS 2

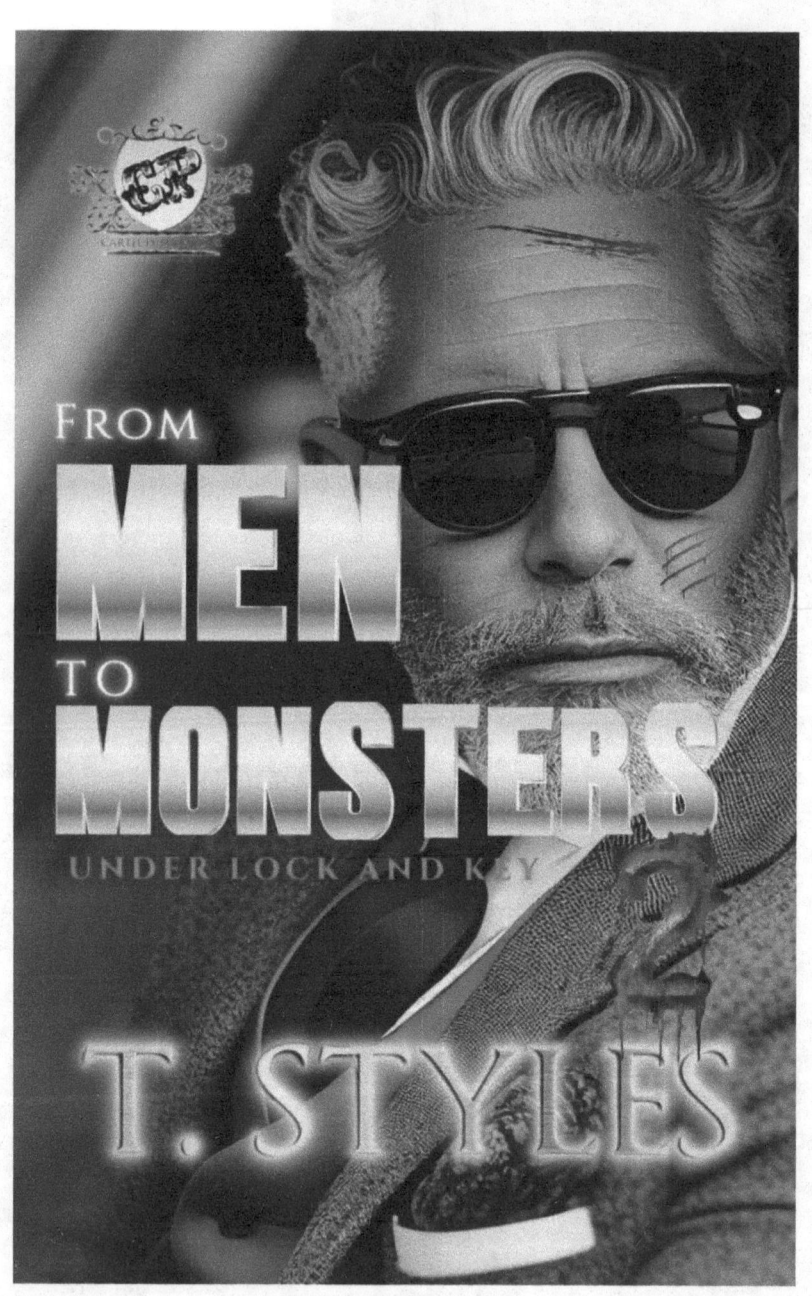

FROM

MEN
TO
MONSTERS

UNDER LOCK AND KEY

T. STYLES

By T. STYLES

ARE YOU ON OUR EMAIL LIST?

SIGN UP ON OUR WEBSITE

www.thecartelpublications.com

Check Out Other Titles By The Cartel Publications

4

By T. Styles

From Men To Monsters 2

PRETTY KINGS 5
FROM MEN TO MONSTERS 2 (WAR 18)
THE END. HOW TO WRITE A BESTSELLING NOVEL IN 30 DAYS

WWW.THECARTELPUBLICATIONS.COM

By T. STYLES

FROM MEN TO MONSTERS 2: UNDER LOCK AND KEY

BY

T. STYLES

Library of Congress Control Number:

ISBN 10:

ISBN 13: 9781948373968

Cover Design: Book Slut Girl

First Edition

Printed in the United States of America

By T. STYLES

WAR SERIES

BOOKS IN ORDER

What up Fam,

It's mid-November, 2024 and as I pen this letter my mood is a little different. If I'm being honest, I'm disappointed in how I looked forward to something happening and it didn't take place. So now, I'm left with the aftermath. Although I feel let down, I have a better outlook than I did a week or so ago, and I realize I have to lean into faith...so I know, no matter what, God got us and we gonna be good! Just try to remember that. #IYKYK

Moving on to a more positive topic, *From Men To Monsters 2: Under Lock & Key!!!!!!!!!!!!!* Babbbbbyyyyyydollllllllll...when I tell you this story had me up all night, I mean just that! I could not put it down until the last word was read! The talented, twisted, T. Styles has once again created another outstanding installment to the wonderful world of Banks Wales & Mason Louisville, and I was left gagged! If you're here on book 18 of this roller coaster that is the War/Truce/Gods/Monsters series, then you already know you about to be in for a nice ride! Make sure you don't burn that Thanksgiving dinner while reading this one! I suggest you put some timers

By T. STYLES

on if you cooking and reading, cuz you gonna need them! LMAO.

Now, let's shift our focus and keep in line with tradition. In this novel, we want to give love to,

KeKe Palmer

Lauren Keyana "KeKe" Palmer is an American actress, talk show and game show host, singer and author. She got her start to the acting business in 2004 at just 11 years old. However, her breakthrough role came just 2 years later when she starred in the blockbuster, *Akeelah and The Bee*. She has been grinding ever since by becoming the youngest talk show host in TV history. As well as the first black woman to star in her own TV show, *True Jackson, VP* on Nickelodeon and the first black woman and the youngest to play Cinderella on Broadway! Although Keke has portrayed many roles, she wowed me by nailing, 'Chili' in the TLC Biopic, *Crazy, Sexy, Cool* and as 'Emerald' in Jordan Peele's thriller, *Nope*!

Now an author, KeKe has pinned her novel, *Master of Me* which is being called, "The most anticipated book of Fall 2024". At the young age of 31, KeKe has already accomplished so much, but I have a feeling we have yet to witness her best! I for one can't wait to see what else Ms. Palmer has up her sleeve!

Aight now, go on! Dive right in and get reacquainted with your favorite crazy families...The Wales' & Louisville's!

Love & Light!

C. Wash
Vice President
The Cartel Publications
www.thecartelpublications.com
www.facebook.com/authortstyles
www.facebook.com/Publishercwash
Instagram: Publishercwash
Instagram: Authortstyles
www.facebook.com/cartelpublications
www.theelitewritersacademy.com
Follow us on IG: Cartelpublications
Follow our Movies on IG: Cartelurbancinema

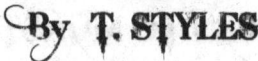

#CartelPublications

#UrbanFiction

#PrayForCece

#KeKePalmer

#FROMMENTOMONSTERS2

By T. STYLES

PROLOGUE
THE PAST

The living room at Sunset Haven buzzed with a swirl of unspoken emotions. Banks, Mason, Patrick, Riot, Bolt, Walid, Blakeslee, Sugar, Minnesota, Spacey, and Joey…who lay in a hospital bed…had settled into a space that was comfortable but laced with unease.

Even though the gang was all there, not everyone was present.

Aliyah, though recovering well, remained in the hospital after sustaining injuries in the explosion at Walid's club.

For now, they found some relief in the security of their new home. The steel doors and advanced systems offered a sense of protection, a fortress against any external threats. Yet that same protection cast a shadow of danger. The thought lingered in their minds: if Banks desired, he could lock each of them inside. No one on the outside would know, nor could they gain access. His obsessive need to keep them safe made them feel profoundly unsafe.

He was back on his bully shit.

Forced smiles flickered across the room, half-hearted attempts to mask the tension. Everyone tried to pretend things were fine, though no one truly believed it. Blakeslee, however, remained silent, her gaze distant and Mason avoided her altogether, unwilling to stir a fragile peace.

Blakeslee's recent sessions at the institution had led to plans for a more permanent stay. Mason knew the weight of the secret they shared, that she had once carried his child, would haunt them both forever. If Banks ever discovered the truth, Mason was certain it would mean the end for them all.

Suddenly, Banks, amid the muted conversations and clinking glasses, surveyed his family. "I'm happy we're all here," he began. "It's been tough, but like Spacey said, honesty and vulnerability will make us the strong unit I know we can be. The Louisville's and the Wales', together as one." The room erupted in cheers.

Mason, glass raised, caught Banks' eye.

"Now, if you don't mind, I'd like some time alone with my old friend."

"Sure, dad," Minnesota replied, her voice soft with affection.

"Whatever you want, pops," Spacey echoed.

As the room emptied, leaving Banks and Mason in the quiet comfort of their sanctuary, Banks moved to the bar with an ease born of countless similar evenings. "Who's thirsty?" He joked, an expensive whiskey in hand.

Mason's response was light, "I am," as he prepared their cigars, a ritual that prefaced their moments in the past.

Seated in their recliners, positioned as always directly across from one another, they settled into the familiarity of their friendship. This setting, whether in Belize, the States, or underground was always the same.

"Everything appears to be going great," Mason observed, breaking the comfortable silence.

"You and I both know that nothing is ever as it seems."

Mason nodded. "True. But it feels like the family understands why we must be here, at least until we find our enemies."

"I agree," Banks concurred. "Until we deal with those on the list, we have to alternate our time from here and above."

"Agreed," Mason nodded.

And then, with a slight shift in tone, posed a question that he wanted and answer to immediately. "But speaking of enemies, can you tell me this...Is it true that you're fucking my daughter, nigga?"

The glass fell from Mason's hand, shattering the peace.

Mason moved to clean it up, but Banks stopped him.

"I'm waiting on an answer," Banks said, his tone sterner.

"I don't know what you mean," Mason tried to maintain his composure.

Banks's eyes narrowed. "So after all these years, you gonna play this game, pretending you don't know what I'm talking about? I've heard things, Mason. I've seen even more."

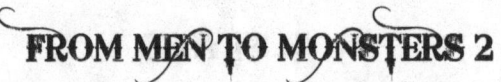

Mason rose, unable to withstand the pressure of Banks's direct questioning.

"Are you sleeping with my daughter?"

Mason took a deep breath, feeling the weight of the inquiry. Despite Blakeslee being a grown woman, he knew the history he shared with Banks ran deep. They had been friends all their lives, bound by a connection that he hoped was still unbreakable and unspoken.

They both understood that they could never be together in a romantic sense, yet their connection was undeniable. A bond so profound it was clear they were soulmates in every way that truly mattered.

And so, Mason feared that admitting the truth might ruin that bond. But hadn't he already crossed that line?

"It's not what you think," Mason said carefully.

"I'm asking you a question," Banks interrupted. "I have given you everything you've ever asked for in life. Because of me you never have to worry about your finances ever again!" He beat his chest.

"And I helped you earn that money too," Mason replied, trying to hold his ground.

"You're not gonna wiggle out of this shit." Banks put down the glass he had been sipping from and rose, his gaze locking onto Mason's.

  By T. STYLES

"Did you sleep with Blakeslee?"

Mason wasn't sure, but it seemed like Banks was beginning to crack at the seams. Would the truth be enough to push him over the edge, condemning them to the lower levels of Sunset Haven forever?

"I need you to look me in my eyes and tell me…are you sleeping with my daughter?"

Mason felt the weight. He knew that if he lied now, he would never get a chance to correct the mistake later. At the same time, he was terrified.

Terrified of losing everything he had.

Terrified of losing him.

He took a deep breath, looked down, and then back into Banks' eyes. "No," he said finally.

Mason wasn't certain, but he thought he saw Banks' body relax, as if hearing the lie brought him some kind of relief. Perhaps Banks felt better knowing Mason had chosen to be deceitful, allowing him to avoid confronting the truth all together.

"Well," Banks said, "I'm having her sent to the institution full-time soon. There's clearly something wrong with her, and I don't want her around anymore."

Mason nodded. "Whatever you want."

Banks' eyes narrowed. "Are you sure about that?"

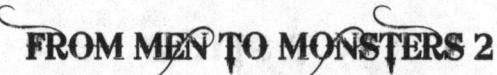

Mason paused, uncertain of what Banks was implying. "I am."

Banks shifted his attention. "Things will get strange over the next few weeks. And not everyone will like how I operate Sunset. But that won't matter as long as I have your support."

Mason nodded. "You do."

"Plus I have it on good authority that an enemy will be trying to approach next week."

"Already?" Mason asked very curious. "Who?"

"Uh...uh...I'll tell you when I get more info."

Mason felt as if he were lying, but why?

"We will be ready when they are," Mason agreed. "But first, let's drink properly. To our unshakable bond."

Banks walked over to the bar, picked up a cool glass, and poured himself another shot of the amber liquid. Next he made Mason a fresh glass since his crashed under the weight of his own lies. He handed it to Mason, who accepted it with a nod.

Raising his glass, Banks lifted it in Mason's direction. "To us."

"To us," Mason repeated, clinking his glass against Banks'.

CHAPTER ONE
TWO WEEKS LATER

Weeks had passed and an enemy was threatening their family. And so they had to retreat to the *down below* permanently, Banks said.

The mood had changed ever since.

Sunset Haven was silent, its sprawling underground halls steeped in a quiet that was both serene and unsettling. The mansion, carved deep beneath the earth, exuded an air of eerie perfection thanks to the Billionaire known as Banks Wales.

Though the house promised luxury, its walls whispered confinement, a new aged prison if you will, where Banks Wales' control reigned supreme.

Who turned on the fucking lights?

Walid stirred awake to an unusual glow filling his room. Aliyah lay asleep beside him, her face soft in the dim light in the luxury hospital bed. Normally, the windows projected moonlight, a setting he had chosen to help Aliyah rest as she recovered from her injuries. But this morning, sunlight streamed through, bright and jarring.

What was going on?

He had better go see.

Walid frowned, sitting up and swinging his legs over the side of the bed. His feet touched the cold porcelain floor, much different from the warmth of the blankets and Aliyah's toasty skin. The small area by the bed was left bare of carpet, allowing for the frame to be rolled easily if needed.

Rising carefully to avoid disturbing Aliyah, the cool, smooth fabric of his midnight-blue silk pajama pants brushed against his skin. As he crossed the room, his toes sank into the plush white carpet, its softness a comforting change from the chill of the floor. Reaching the door, he grasped the handle and gave it a firm pull.

It didn't budge.

He tried again, this time with more force. Nothing.

"Fuck is going on?" He said, his voice barely above a whisper.

The thought of Banks' omnipotent control over the mansion never left his mind. It was a reality that haunted him nightly, though he tried to hide it, especially from Aliyah. And now he was getting proof that his fears were warranted.

"Is everything okay?" Aliyah's soft voice came from behind him.

 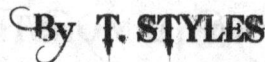

Walid turned to her, quickly replacing his concern with a reassuring smile. "Everything's fine, baby," he said, easing back into bed. He wrapped his arms around her, pulling her close so her face could rest against his chest. "Go back to sleep."

As her lids closed, he stared at the door with a fixed gaze.

Others would soon meet him in his quieted rage.

In another part of the house, wearing a black Versace embroidered robe, Mason was already up, pounding on his door with the palm of his hand. Like Walid, he found himself locked in, the sunlight streaming through his window feeling more like mind games than warmth. The knowledge that Sunset Haven was an underground fortress designed to "protect" them, was really to keep them in line.

This shit only deepened his frustration.

But he was not alone.

Throughout the mansion, the same scene played out. Riot, Banks' grandson, yanked at his door to no avail. Minnesota and her young niece, Sugar, met the same fate, their doors unyielding. Bolt and Patrick, Mason's son and grandson, also found themselves trapped. Everyone was locked in, the quiet hum of the house suddenly feeling like prison.

And then, just as certain as the doors had locked, they clicked open.

One by one, the family emerged from their rooms, moving like sleepwalkers toward the breakfast room. No one was hungry, but curiosity and unease propelled them forward. They needed fucking answers.

There they found the master, Banks, seated at the head of the long dining table, a lavish breakfast spread laid out before him. His black pajama shirt hung open, revealing a hint of his toned chest, while his salt-and-pepper grey hair framed his striking, handsome face, exuding a commanding yet effortless presence.

The family was mad as mad could be and yet the aroma of freshly baked pastries and sizzling bacon filled the air, but no one felt the comfort such a meal might usually bring.

"Why were the doors locked?" Walid demanded, his voice firm but calm. He scratched his short cropped curly hair.

All eyes turned to Banks, waiting for an explanation. His smile was disarming, but there was a chill behind it that none of them missed. "It was a mistake," he said lightly, his tone betraying no hint of remorse. "Something in the control panels I guess. It's fixed though."

Mason wasn't convinced. "You don't make mistakes," he said, his voice laced with suspicion. "You make moves."

"Yeah, pops," Spacey chimed in as he stepped into the room, his eyes narrowing. "What's really going on? A shawty I was playing hide and seek with thought I was trying to keep her hostage."

"Were you?" Minnesota said. "I don't know why you keep hiding in that unfinished ass bathroom."

"Shut up…it makes me feel like I'm slumming." He waved his sister off.

Banks leaned back in his chair, his smile never faltering. "Like I said, everything is fine. I won't massage your emotions again. Now come. Eat. Or would you prefer I eat alone?" His tone grew sharper, his words carrying a subtle menace. "Before you give your answer, please remember that I hate eating alone." He picked up a piece of bacon and broke it apart. "It puts me in somewhat of a bad mood."

There was a pause, the tension in the room thick enough to choke on. Reluctantly, they each took their seats around the table. Whether out of fear, duty, or the need to watch him closely, they gave him their full attention.

And obedience.

It was all he wanted.

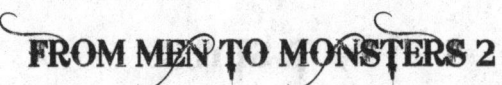

LATER THAT DAY

The halls of Sunset Haven were quiet, save for the soft clink of ice against a glass as Banks swirled the amber liquid in his hand. The faint scent of his whiskey, smokey and sharp, lingered in the air as he moved slowly through the dimly lit corridors.

No shirt, just white linen pants, his salt-and-pepper hair glinted slightly under the soft light. As he observed a home of his own design, he smiled. It was a reminder of the years of control and power he wielded...but also the isolation left behind. Who needed Belize when you could create your own underground fortress?

If only people could be happy.

Even Mason seemed to avoid him these days.

Would he leave him too?

Banks had no destination in mind as he wandered around. His grip on the glass tightened when he walked up to Mason's office and heard the muffled sound of his voice.

He paused, tilting his head closer to the door.

By T. STYLES

"Blakeslee, you doing okay?" His tone was gentle, warm, and filled with concern. "I know that place is hard on you, but... you'll get through it. He says you have to spend three days there and the rest here," There was a pause. "You can be angry all you want, but I must check on you." Another pause. "From what I'm told he'll bring you back. Just be honest with the therapists."

A fucking traitor!

Banks glared into the darkness.

Though the words were innocent, they ignited fury deep inside his soul. He clenched his jaw, his mind conjuring a thousand reasons to distrust Mason's intentions. The glass in his hand trembled slightly as he downed the rest of the whiskey in one swift motion, letting the burn trail down his throat.

Pushing himself away from the door, Banks continued down the hall, upon another set of voices.

It was Walid and his tone was low, heavy and filled with emotion.

"He was a monster, but I miss him so much," Walid said quietly. Banks moved closer, his footsteps soft, and peered inside his open doorway. Walid sat on the couch in his room, his elbows on his knees, hands clasped as if in prayer. Aliyah was on the bed and looked over at him with longing eyes, wanting to do something to help him but knowing she couldn't.

"He was my brother…and no matter what I will always fucking love him."

"I know," she said softly. "And Ace loved you too. You were his twin. Nothing…and I do mean nothing can ever change that. Not even your father."

"I know, baby."

"I just wish we could leave this place. I liked it better up there. This feels so dark."

"Did he call again?" Walid asked.

"Josh? Yes. Why?"

"I'm just asking."

"Don't worry, Walid. I want you and only you. I want our family to work too. And when I'm well enough to move around again, I'll show you. Maybe we can even get a place of our own."

"Yeah…maybe."

Banks' chest tightened as he took in the scene, his son's grief out in the open for all to hear. A wave of jealousy surged through him, bitter and unrelenting.

As far as he could tell, no one had ever spoken about him with such tenderness. No one grieved for him as they did for Ace.

And leaving Sunset?

Why leave when the place had every high-tech experience imaginable?

Slowly he moved on, his steps heavier now. Passing another room, Banks stopped again at the sound of laughter. Bolt and Patrick were sprawled out on the floor, their voices carrying a carefree energy that only deepened the ache in Banks' chest.

"Man, Ace was so cool," Bolt said, shaking his head and grinning. "You remember when he took us all out that night? And let us bust our guns. I mean your shot was off but mine was steady."

"I know you lying!" Patrick snapped. "I just ain't feel like busting that day," He sighed. "Anyway, Ace had his problems, but he was one of us. But Banks and them niggas always like throwing people away."

Banks didn't wait to hear more. His breath felt caught in his tattooed chest, his vision filled with acts of revenge.

Every room, every conversation, every whispered memory was about someone else.

Ace. Mason. Anyone but him.

He was the villain in his own castle, and he hated that shit.

Gripping the empty glass tightly, he stormed back toward his office and once there, he shoved the heavy door open. The cool, stale air of the room greeted him like an unwelcome guest.

Standing in the middle of his doorway, he looked out into the house. His breath rose and fell even more in his chest, before he slammed it with one hand.

CHAPTER TWO

Quinn Harley walked into Joey's room, her presence soft yet steady. Joey lay motionless, unable to move his body on his own due to the hit taken out on his family. Joey was injured when he was pushed into traffic by a person meaning to do the Wales family harm. And as a result he could only move his neck and head.

Quinn was at his beck and call, but in his opinion she was too beautiful to be merely a nurse. Joey felt she was a prop put in place by Banks since Joey was a former addict. Banks needed to ensure that the medicines Joey now needed would not be abused. Despite Joey's feeling of why she was there, she seemed very skilled at handling his care. Her shoulder-length blonde hair framed her face, and her piercing blue eyes seemed focused entirely on him whenever she was in the room. Today was no different.

"Good morning, Mr. Wales," she said gently, "you don't have to say it to me."

"What's good about today?" Joey responded, his tone edged with frustration. "It's bad enough that you're hired to take pity on me."

She smiled, undeterred, and moved over to the dresser. Picking up the remote control, she pressed several buttons, transforming the blank walls around them into a stunning scene of windows overlooking a beach. The image was so vivid Joey almost felt he could smell the ocean air.

Quinn placed the remote down and walked over to the sink before grabbing the basin and filling it with warm water. Then, reaching for the soap and a washcloth, she returned to his bedside.

"I'm never going to treat you like anything other than a person, and my boss," she said softly. "Because that's what you are. Pity is not even an idea for me."

She leaned over, carefully removing his shirt. Dipping the washcloth in the warm water, she started to wash his honey brown body. Beginning with his face and moving to his neck, arms, and chest.

When a strand of her hair brushed against his cheek, Joey turned his gaze away, unable to meet her eyes.

"Sorry about that," she said tucking the strands behind her ear.

He couldn't deny the care she seemed to have for him felt authentic. A part of him felt undeserving. After all, he'd made mistakes, chosen the wrong people, trusted the wrong hearts. One of those choices had led to a woman he trusted setting him up, leaving him to be hit by a truck in the middle of the road.

Broken and alone.

In his mind what could he offer someone now?

Quinn continued, wiping down his belly, then moving to his private areas, legs, and feet. She was gentle, taking her time as if to remind him he was still human despite his injuries. When she finished, she carefully dried him off and rubbed lotion onto his skin before helping him into fresh clothes.

Joey's bed was top of the line, able to lift him into a seated position with ease. And so she did. In the upright position, he felt, well, human. This made it simpler for Quinn to bring over his wheelchair and assist him as he settled into it.

"I wish you'd stop doing everything for me," he muttered, a touch of vulnerability in his voice.

She giggled. "So I can lose my job? No, thank you. I don't know why, but I have a feeling this family needs me. That you need me."

He took a deep breath as she prepared to wheel him out for the meeting Banks had called. But just before they left the room, the door creaked open, and a small figure slipped inside.

It was six-year-old Sugar Wales.

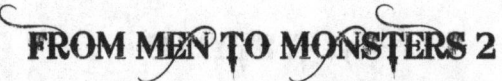

FROM MEN TO MONSTERS 2   33

Sugar, the birth daughter to Blakeslee Wales was being raised by Minnesota, her sister. And so Sugar considered her aunt to be her mother.

The girl moved with a practiced lightness, her steps barely audible on the polished floor. Her pigtails bouncing playfully. She was a pro at taking things she wanted, and her room was a collection of such. On a mission, her wide, curious eyes darted to Joey's bedside table, where a small, intricate snow globe sat. It was a gift from Minnesota, one of the few personal touches in his otherwise sterile space.

While they were busy, Sugar reached out and scooped up the globe with delicate fingers. She turned it over in her hands, shaking it lightly to make the glitter swirl inside.

And as they continued their conversation, she disappeared.

When Joey was all cleaned she looked at him.

"Ready."

"Let's go," Quinn said, shaking her head while pushing Joey's wheelchair toward the door.

"To tell you the truth I don't feel like it."

"I hear you, but I don't want you to be late for this meeting Banks called."

Quinn, sensing his mood changed, stopped and leaned over slightly. "What you thinking about?" She asked.

 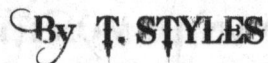 **By T. STYLES**

"Nothing." Joey said quickly, though his mind was still on Quinn and how well she cared for him.

Quinn let out a soft laugh. "By the way, Joey I don't pity you. I consider you a man. A very handsome one at that. Maybe you should start treating yourself a little better…and give me a chance."

With that, she began to push him slowly down the hall, but her words lingered in his mind.

Give me a chance.

What did she mean by that?

CHAPTER THREE

Blakeslee sat at her vanity, brushing her long, dark hair as she studied her reflection. The bristles of the gold-handled brush ended in tiny beads, glinting as she moved them through her black locks. The light caused her vanilla skin to sparkle.

Truth be told she secretly wished that someone would finally recognize her for the woman she was trying to be…and not the evil mischievous thoughts that always covered her mind.

She was in a rhythm but paused as the door swung open without a knock, a break from the usual beauty protocol. When the door fully opened, she didn't need to turn to know who it was. Only her father would be so disrespectful.

Setting the brush down gently on the quilted pearl pillow beside her, Blakeslee looked up, meeting her father's gaze in the mirror.

"Father," she said, her voice cool.

He stepped into the room, his expression stern. "You aren't well."

She frowned, taken aback. "I've been better, but I don't know what you're getting at."

"I've spoken to your doctors," he replied, his tone sharp. "Why do you entertain thoughts of patricide?"

"I believe it's matricide that makes me smile."

"Don't fuck with me!"

She stiffened. "Well, first of all, that's against the rules for them to tell you my —"

"Stop it." He waved his hand dismissively, cutting her off. "I don't want to hear any more of your lies. I will keep this family safe, from everyone, including you. Because I can tell that the only thing you care about is destroying me."

"What if it's you that's putting everyone in danger? Because no one has ever been scared of little old me."

"You are to stay in that place full time."

"No! Please don't do this, father! You all are all I have."

"It's done."

Blakeslee looked at him intently. This was about something else. "You believe me," she said quietly, an edge to her voice. "Don't you? About me and your best friend."

Banks inhaled sharply. "If you're preparing to tell lies, I won't hear it."

"I'm not lying. I had a relationship with your precious fucking Mason. And it went deeper than he will ever admit. I kissed him. Sucked him. Fucked him. And so much more."

"What is wrong with you?" Banks said, his voice rising. "Why can't peace be good enough for you? Why do you always have to cause trouble?"

"Because I'm just like you. I see you're losing weight. I see the hate in your eyes. You're losing control aren't you, *father*?" Tears began to well in her eyes, but she held his gaze. "Before long, everyone will leave you too."

She rose and stood across from him.

"I'm still your little girl, whether you like it or not! But here I am, being honest and you hate me so much that even when I speak the truth, a truth you're fully aware of, you prefer to use it against me to keep me away."

"You are a lesion on my name."

Her head dropped as she pushed back a few strands of hair, tucking them behind her ear. She straightened, looking at him with resolve. "Until you do right by how you treat me, and Ace, nothing ever good will happen to you."

Quickly he rushed up to her and smacked her hard. The sound remained long after the wound was caused.

"I'll get the help, but I won't let you push me away this time. I have been praying on your downfall. For you to finally get what you deserve. And this time I think God is listening."

"Be careful with—."

"I will be a part of this family, whether I'm sick or in perfect health." Her voice softened. "After all, that is the Wales fucking way, isn't it?"

He glared at her for a moment, then turned toward the door. "Get dressed and come to the meeting."

Blakeslee watched as he took one last look at her before leaving, when the door closed she fell to her knees.

CHAPTER FOUR

Walid was asleep in the bed he shared with Aliyah. The room was dark, silent except for her occasional soft moan, something he had grown accustomed to hearing since her injury. Despite the battle scars on her face, she was still stunning. Her light brown skin, due to her Belizean heritage caused her to look like she was glowing.

Just being next to him kept him at peace.

For him, taking care of her now felt like nursing a small broken bird back to health. He regarded every limb of her body as fragile, weak, and had pledged to make her strong once again.

Still, it was time to awaken.

Careful not to disturb her too much, he slipped out of bed, turned on the light, and moved to the side of the bed. Kneeling beside her, he took her hand and looked into her eyes as they fluttered open. Her face, still bruised from the explosion at his nightclub, mirrored the pain she carried.

"How you feel?" He asked softly.

She smiled and squeezed his hand. "The way you look at me…"

"What you mean?" He grinned.

"With all the fighting we used to do, it just feels good to have you look at me this way."

"Which way?"

"With love." She tried to shift herself into a sitting position, but her strength failed her.

Without hesitation, he stood up, and pushed a button on the bed to help her move erect. Then he took a seat beside her placing a warm hand on her leg.

"Are you in a lot of pain?" He asked gently. "I mean, you don't have to attend this meeting my father hosting."

"Of course I do. Plus, I need to talk to him."

"About what?" He asked, his tone cautious.

"About... you know who," she replied, her voice soft. "Josh Fisher."

"Oh...your ex." Walid's expression darkened. He was tired of dealing with the person who had infiltrated their relationship. A person who only gained the opportunity because a while back, Walid was too much like his dad and wanted her to come running back to him.

"He's not an ex because we never made things official. But he is a man with power. And things were said that I think he won't let go."

"He called you today?" He asked, jaw tightening.

"He never stops."

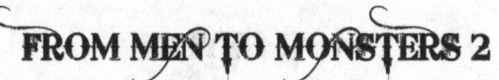

"This is why you should just let me put him out his misery," Walid said, his voice firm. "Then we could be done with this once and for all."

"Walid," she replied, "I need you to love me, not control all things that happen in my life. Remember, your need for control is the reason we're in this situation in the first place. Be better than your father."

He looked down, feeling the sting of her words.

"I just want to talk to your father," she continued, "to make sure he's aware of any potential problems. For all we know it might not matter."

Walid took a deep breath, shifting the subject. "I hear you."

"Did Banks say what he wants to talk to us about?"

"It's the list from Sharon Drexel," he replied. "He wants to go over the people on it."

"What list?"

"The enemy list."

Suddenly her temples throbbed. "And then what happens?" Her voice trailed off. "Will our lives change even more? Because I've never seen a man hold more power on humans than he has…except a prison warden."

By T. STYLES

Walid had some ideas but he wasn't about to burden her with them. "Let me get you some medicine." He stood and walked away.

CHAPTER FIVE

Patrick and Bolt were in the gym, doing presses on the three available benches. Bolt was pleased with his current weight arrangement, but Patrick wanted to level up. So after finishing his set, he sat up, sweat dripping down his brown face. "I need you to come over here and check me when you finish that," he said, watching Bolt.

Bolt didn't look up. "Actually, I'm doing more than one rep."

"I want you to spot me now," Patrick replied, "you not even lifting nothing heavy for real."

Bolt shook his head. "Like I was saying, I'm busy."

Lately Bolt had been bucking back. Something he never did before and it was angering him. Annoyed, Patrick jumped up and walked toward him. "What's up with you lately?"

Bolt struggled under the weight for a moment before answering, "What you mean, *what's up with me?*"

"You been real standoffish," Patrick pressed. "And I'm not feeling that shit."

Bolt chuckled dryly. "I don't know what you talking about. I'm not your slave. So I don't have to jump when you call."

He may have faked dumb, but Bolt knew exactly what Patrick was talking about. Ever since Riot, who they'd both low-key bullied for years, placed a wig on Patrick's head in defiance before whipping his ass, Bolt started to feel that he could defy Patrick too. The incident stripped Patrick of the intimidating aura he once possessed. He was no longer the "big bad wolf" everyone thought he was.

He was...well...a bitch.

Patrick sensed this change, but he chose not to confront it directly. Instead, he did what he always did. Bully Bolt to assert his dominance. And so, when Bolt rose to start on another machine, Patrick shoved him from behind. Bolt stumbled forward. Unable to stop his feet from moving from up under his body, he went crashing into the wall.

"How 'bout you push me like you just pushed him," a voice called out from the doorway.

Patrick and Bolt turned to see Riot entering the gym. His long, silky hair cascaded down his back, and his light skin seemed to glisten with tiny flecks of silver. Riot took care of his mind and body, but more importantly, he was at peace with the young man he was starting to become.

Riot moved deeper inside the family gym.

Although undeniably pretty, he was straight, and he carried himself with a rare confidence that combined both strength and beauty, making him all the more alluring.

"You fucking with people again?" Riot asked, directing his gaze at Patrick.

"Man, I ain't got time for —" Patrick began, but Riot cut him off.

"I asked you a question," Riot said firmly.

Bolt smiled from the background, finding satisfaction in the moment.

"You know what, fuck this gym," Patrick whispered, avoiding Riot's stare.

Riot nodded, as Patrick disappeared. Once he was gone, Riot turned to Bolt. "You better start standing up for yourself."

"I don't know what you talking about," Bolt replied, laughing it off.

"He's your nephew but he's not your friend. He'll never be your friend. You'll find that out sooner or later," Riot said, his voice steady. "Let's go. It's time for the meeting."

Bolt looked down, absorbing Riot's words, then followed him out of the gym.

CHAPTER SIX

Banks was seated in the living room beside a fake fireplace that cast an amber glow, flickering softly to mimic real flames. The room was arranged with plush armchairs and leather sofas, but as his family members filed in, no one seemed inclined to sit. An unspoken tension filled the space, thickening the air with an uneasy silence.

With everyone gathered, including Blakeslee, Banks took a deep breath and spoke, his voice steady and firm. "Lorna, you can come out now."

A woman emerged from the shadows, her steps slow and deliberate, followed by ten imposing strangers. They were dressed in all black Hakama styled uniforms. Their expressions were unreadable, faces set like stone, eyes scanning the room.

The all black made Lorna, who was clearly the leader, look as if she was wearing white face paint. Her light skin was littered with strawberry-colored freckles and her hair was pulled into a tight bun that sat on top of her head. She was black but could be considered albino if she was one shade closer to the moon.

Mason, standing near the back, frowned, confusion and suspicion flashing across his face.

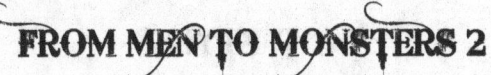

Banks cleared his throat. "Lorna will be head of security," he announced. "Her men have been vetted and will be responsible for keeping you safe when you're out of the house. They are not meant to speak to you, so if you try, they will say nothing. But they will go with you. Everywhere."

Spacey glanced over at Minnesota, then back at his father, his eyebrows raised. "What exactly you doing, pops?" He asked, voice low but tense. "I mean, did something happen you haven't told us about yet?"

Banks leaned forward, his gaze unwavering. "We've located the threat," he replied. "And this time, the most present threat is... Josh Fisher."

Aliyah's chest locked on her, causing her breathing to hurry.

A hush fell over the room as Aliyah immediately lowered her head, a flicker of recognition crossing her face. She knew exactly who he was. A man who, despite her feelings for Walid, believed she was being held here against her will.

"Who's Josh?" Minnesota asked, her brow furrowed.

Banks turned to Aliyah. "Do you want to tell them," he asked, his tone unyielding, "or should I?"

Aliyah inhaled deeply, her voice barely more than a whisper. "When I thought Walid and I weren't going to make it, I... I started dating. Josh was almost a boyfriend but not really."

"Oh...the lawyer," Minnesota responded.

From across the room, Walid's fists clenched, his knuckles turning white as he held them stiffly behind his back, noticing the glances from his family. He kept his expression controlled, but a spark of anger for Josh and everything he represented held strong behind his eyes.

"I don't want to be bothered with him anymore," Aliyah continued, her tone thick with frustration, "but he won't leave me alone. Until he sees me."

"So let the nigga look," Spacey said. "So we can be free of it all."

"I'm not putting her in danger," Walid said.

"I think that's smart, son," Mason added. "Especially if he's really a threat."

Banks glared. "You sound like you don't believe me."

"I never said that."

Spacey exhaled, his arms crossing over his chest. "So you think this guy more powerful than us?"

Banks's gaze hardened. "If I thought he was more powerful we wouldn't have the men that we have. This isn't

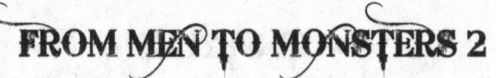

about fear; it's about safety. It would be easier for me if I felt that each of you would listen and follow orders… but we all know how that goes. At any rate, Lorna and her team are here to make sure that changes."

Suddenly, Mason wrinkled his nose, glancing around in mild disgust. "Hold up… what's that smell?"

"I smelled it too but I ain't wanna call it," Spacey said.

Lorna sighed, crossing her arms, unbothered by his reaction. "I don't wash regularly. Or use deodorant," she said. "Once a month is my schedule, usually."

Spacey suppressed a laugh, shaking his head in disbelief. "You have got to be kidding me."

"I'm not," Lorna replied, stepping forward without a hint of shame. The odor now stronger. "I'm due for a shower in a few days, if that makes things easier. But let me be clear, I'm the best at what I do. Soon you'll all see too."

Mason raised an eyebrow, skeptical. "And what exactly do you do?"

Lorna's eyes narrowed, her voice turning steely. "I make sure people live long enough to see their bloodline grow. I make sure people live beyond a calendar year. And I will admit, some might not like my methods, but my track record speaks for itself. From the children of U.S. presidents

By T. STYLES

to the wives of dictators around the world, they all have me to thank that their hearts still beat strong."

She was very spooky.

Lorna swept her eyes over the room, her expression challenging. "And if you're lucky enough to have me on your side, you'll be here to tell the story of how I saved your lives too."

Banks picked up his glass of whiskey, the ice cubes clinking softly as he swirled them. His glare was sharp, and his tone carried a warning as he spoke. "These people are here for all of us. If it's a problem, I have other ways to make sure my instructions are followed."

"And what's that?" Mason said. "Accidently close the doors again?"

Banks laughed, causing it to echo throughout the house.

After the meeting, Banks strolled leisurely down the hallway, a golf club resting over his shoulder and a glass of whiskey in his free hand. Walid appeared behind him, his silhouette tall and imposing.

"Father," he said softly.

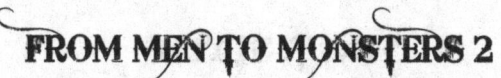

For a moment, Banks slowed, tilting his head vaguely as if assessing his son's approach. Walid stopped directly in front of him, his chest heaving slightly, though his voice was measured when he spoke.

"Father, can we talk?"

"About what?"

"I'm concerned about you."

Banks smirked, swirling the whiskey in his glass. "Concerned? You got me confused with Baltimore or something?"

Walid sighed. "I've seen what this house...is doing to you. Doing to us. And if there's anything I can do, just... let me."

Banks' eyes narrowed. "That's sweet, Ace. But I don't need anyone to take care of me. Least of all you."

The word stopped Walid in his tracks. "Ace?" He repeated, his voice dropping to a whisper. His jaw tightened as he stared at his father, his chest rising and falling with quick, shallow breaths. "I'm not Ace, father."

Banks stared at him for a long moment, the silence stretching between them like a taut wire. His expression didn't falter, didn't shift, as though the words hadn't even registered. "You know what I mean."

By T. STYLES

Walid turned to leave but then gripped Banks in a hug, before pushing him away and walking off.

Banks stood poised on the artificial green, preparing for his swing in the golf range he had meticulously designed. Although they were underground, the space felt remarkably lifelike. The grass beneath his feet was vivid and lush, perfectly groomed and each wall displayed a seamless projection of a bright blue sky, complete with soft, drifting clouds and a radiant sun.

Focused, Banks angled his club behind the ball, eyes narrowed as he assessed the distance.

Suddenly, Mason's hurried footsteps broke the silence as he approached from behind. "What the fuck is you doing?" He demanded. "The *having niggas follow us around* routine never works!"

Banks didn't glance up. He studied the ball a moment longer before giving it a light, calculated tap with the club. "You know exactly what I'm doing," he replied coolly, watching the ball roll smoothly across the green.

"Why has it come to this again?" Mason's voice was serious, almost pleading. "We been here before, man. Why you putting your children through this again?"

Banks exhaled sharply, tightening his grip on the club. He aligned himself for another shot. "You want me to say it in another language? I'm doing this to keep you all safe."

With a sturdy but confident swag, he brought the club back and swung again, his body moving with precision. The sound of the club connecting with the ball filled the air with a satisfying crack. All it did was piss Mason off even more because the nigga hardly ever missed.

Mason shook his head, his face etched with frustration. "I don't agree with this," he said firmly. "Not for your kids or mine. They're adults, Banks. It's time you start treating them that way."

"I'm sending Blakeslee away…to get more help."

"Why you telling me?"

Banks laughed.

Annoyed, Mason turned to leave, but Banks' voice stopped him in his tracks.

"You owe me."

Mason turned back, brows furrowed. "I owe you?"

"Yes, Mason." Banks' tone was steady but pointed, each word weighted. He looked up, his eyes meeting Mason's,

 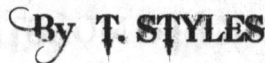

holding his gaze with an intensity that left no room for argument. "And without going into too much detail, I think you know exactly what I mean."

A tense silence hung between them.

Banks straightened, resting the club on his shoulder. "Now, unless you're here to play against me," he said, a slight smirk tugging at the corner of his mouth, "I'd prefer if you left me the fuck alone."

Mason chuckled under his breath. "I hear you, Warden Wales," he said, storming off.

Blakeslee sat silently in the passenger seat of the Maybach as it glided down the smooth, dimly lit road. Beside her, the quiet hum of the engine blended with the subtle scent of leather and a faint trace of her own rose scented perfume.

To pass the time, she glanced out the window, watching the darkened streets slip by, then looked briefly at her driver. In the far back seat, her handler sat, as silent as her father had promised. He hadn't spoken a word to her the entire drive.

She studied her driver once more, noting the familiar lines of his profile. He'd been with her on and off for a long time. A man of few words himself, she trusted him more than she trusted her father or this cold-eyed handler.

"Does this seem right to you?" She asked quietly, her voice carrying a note of uncertainty.

The driver gave her a quick glance before looking away. "You know I stay out of your affairs," he replied, his words carefully neutral.

She pressed, her voice soft but firm. "But you're human. You're not a robot. So humor a sad little girl."

"You're a grown woman now."

She smiled. "There he is."

The driver wanted to say more but hesitated, his eyes flickering in the rearview mirror before he answered. "Even if I wanted to speak to you about what you're asking… is right now the right time?" He tilted his head ever so slightly toward the back and Blakeslee understood.

She turned in her seat, her gaze meeting the icy stare of the man behind her. There was something in his presence that sent a chill through her. He was here to ensure her safety, so her father claimed. But as she sat there, the car moving steadily toward the institution, a dark thought crept into her mind.

If this man was supposed to keep her alive, why did she suddenly feel an overwhelming sense of danger?

Blakeslee took a deep breath, turning back to face forward. She didn't know what lay ahead, but one thing was certain, she had no intention of taking any of this lightly.

Not this time.

This family was going to learn to respect her or else.

CHAPTER SEVEN

R iot stood in front of his mirror, brushing his long, silky hair. His movements were slow and careful, each stroke giving his reflection a calm, collected air. As he worked, he noticed Bolt entering the room quietly. Riot turned, meeting Bolt's gaze with a slight smile, then gestured to the chair beside him.

"Sit down," Riot said in a welcoming tone.

Bolt, accustomed to Patrick's harsh, bullying ways, felt a surprising wave of relief at the warmth in Riot's voice. He settled into the chair, his shoulders visibly relaxing.

"Are you scared?" Bolt asked, his voice barely more than a murmur.

"About what?" Riot replied, still focused on his hair.

"You know, everything going on with Banks." Bolt's question was laced with worry. "Do you really think he'll have someone following us wherever we go?"

Riot paused, setting his brush down on the dresser. He took a deep breath and moved to lean against the wall, crossing his arms before letting them fall naturally to his sides. His physique had become lean and defined from his recent workout routines, and the muscles cut sharply under his vanilla-toned skin.

"I don't know what's going on with grandfather," he admitted. "But I'm not really worried, to tell you the truth. All I know is, if we stay out of the way and keep from making noise or causing problems, we'll be fine. And those who choose to get in the way while the elders do their thing, always get touched."

Bolt sighed, glancing around the room. "You know what I don't get?"

Riot shook his head, waiting for Bolt to continue.

"There's so much money in this family," Bolt said, a hint of frustration in his voice. "But nobody ever seems happy. We have all these nice things, and we can go anywhere we want…but nobody goes anywhere. And that scares me."

Riot stepped closer, placing a reassuring hand on Bolt's shoulder. His grip was firm, steady. "Listen, we're going to be okay," he said, his voice strong. "I know it doesn't feel like it, but we will be. Let's just do what he wants us to do for now. If at any point I feel like it's unsafe for you or me, I'll be the first to let you know."

Bolt looked up at him, eyes filled with hope. "You promise?"

"I got you," Riot replied with a nod.

Just then, Patrick appeared in the doorway, his expression unreadable as he looked between them. "I was

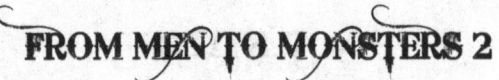

going to play that new video game, Bolt," he said, though his eyes were fixed on Riot before he quickly glanced away. "You wanna play with me?"

Bolt turned to Riot, a silent question in his eyes. "Actually...I was gonna hang out here for a little while."

Patrick's gaze darkened as he looked at them both, then, without another word, walked away, leaving a heavy silence in his wake.

Banks sat cross-legged on the plush living room carpet, the rich hues of the intricate rug soft beneath him. Across from him, Sugar knelt with a childish grin, clutching a handful of cards that barely fit in her small hands. "Do you have any kings?" She asked, her voice sweet and eager. Banks smirked, holding up a single card before handing it over with exaggerated reluctance.

"You're too good at this," he said, his tone warm and indulgent. Sugar giggled, her laughter echoing through the room as she added the card to her growing pile. He didn't need to know about the cards under her lap. It was her little secret.

By T. STYLES

The scene was almost surreal…her joy, so pure, softened even the hard lines of Banks' face.

Not everyone thought the shit was precious though.

Just beyond the doorway, members of the family passed by their expressions ranging from disbelief to simmering anger. Minutes earlier, Banks had delivered harsh ass orders, his voice cold and commanding, leaving no room for dissent.

Now, here he was, playing a simple card game like they both wore pigtails with no care in the world. To them, he was a tyrant, a man who thrived on control and manipulation.

But to Sugar, he was a hero.

She saw none of the monster they did, only a grandfather who made time to play Go Fish and let her win every round. The sight was both maddening and heartbreaking, leaving the family seething as they moved on.

Banks sat up from his massage table, feeling the lingering warmth from the deep tissue work as he pulled on

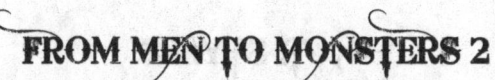

his plush red robe. He gave a nod to his therapist for a job well done. "Thank you, Betsy."

Making his exit, the sound of footsteps alerted him, and he turned to see his children, Minnesota and Spacey, standing nearby. As he walked past them, he gave a small smile.

"I figured you'd be out in the streets," he remarked, a trace of humor in his voice. "Considering how much you hate it here."

"You mean on the double dates you set up for us with them niggas?"

Banks laughed.

Spacey exchanged a quick glance with Minnesota, then turned back to his father. "Anyway I didn't say I hate it here. I just feel like...like this place is our casket."

Banks let out a quiet sigh, shaking his head. "Always so melodramatic," he responded. "You don't know what a casket is until you live in the projects of Baltimore city."

The three of them moved down the corridor, the cool marble beneath their feet giving way to a faint scent of chlorine as they neared the indoor pool. Once inside, Banks shrugged off his robe, draping it over a nearby chair before easing himself into the bubbling hot tub. Steam rose around him as he moaned in satisfaction.

"So," he said, leaning back and stretching his arms along the edge of the tub. "Let's hear it. What do you want with me now?"

Minnesota frowned, crossing her arms. "What do we want? You called us here."

Banks glared, the look of amusement fading from his face. "No, I didn't."

"Yes, you did, pops," Spacey interjected. "You told us to come here because you wanted to talk about what all this means for the family. The handlers and Lorna's funky ass. You don't remember that shit?"

For a brief instance, a flicker of uncertainty crossed Banks' face. He wasn't cocky for the moment, his expression now replaced with worry. But just as quickly, he cleared his throat, his posture straightening, and his expression hardened.

"Oh, yeah," he said, regaining his usual authority. "I remember."

Minnesota and Spacey exchanged a glance.

"And you can stop all the glancing at each other shit too," Banks said. "It's annoying at best."

They didn't realize he noticed.

"I know neither of you like the current situation," Banks began, calm but firm. "But I need you to talk to the others.

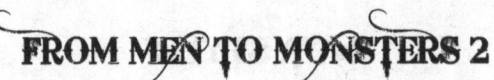

Make them as comfortable as possible. This is the new world, and we're going to adapt to it until I say otherwise."

Minnesota shook her head, frustration evident on her face. "So how am I supposed to make anyone comfortable when I'm not?"

"Exactly," Spacey added, leaning against the wall.

Banks shook his head. "I know you both hate that you were born into the Wales family, but this is our reality. Our way of life." He took a deep breath, the jets of the hot tub humming softly as he spoke. "Over time, I'm one hundred percent certain that things will get better. Tell them that, make them understand. The moment you believe it they will too."

Minnesota's eyes narrowed slightly, determination in her face. "You know what, I'm gonna just come out with it."

"Don't do it," Spacey said under his breath.

"Father, I want to talk to you about having my own place again."

Banks met her gaze steadily. "And I've already told you, if you feel you want to leave, go. But you will not be taking Sugar."

Minnesota's face tightened, a glimmer of defiance in her eyes. He knew that was the one person she wasn't willing to let go. "Why?"

By T. STYLES

"She's safer here with me," Banks stated, his tone final.

"You sure about that?" She replied.

Spacey, watching the exchange, hesitated before speaking up. "Well, what if I wanted to leave? Could I go? With my son."

Banks chuckled softly, leaning his head back and closing his eyes. "I see you're both in a mood for games. But I just had my massage, so I'm not. Leave me be."

Mason waited anxiously in the hallway, waving Walid, Spacey, and Minnesota into his room with an urgent gesture. Once they were all inside, he cast a quick look down the hall, then closed the door quietly, locking it behind him.

"What we gonna do?" Spacey asked, his voice breaking the tense silence. "Something's off with him!"

"I don't know," Mason replied, moving to the artificial window that overlooked a fabricated skyline. The illusion was so convincing it almost felt real, but he knew better. He turned back toward the others. "But I think we might have to consider leaving."

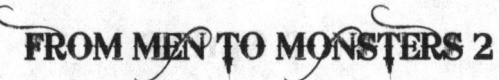

"You mean escaping," Spacey corrected him.

"How do we even do that, Mason? I been trying to leave with Sugar but he won't let me."

"You know how close he is to Sugar, Minnesota. In his mind, she doesn't give him trouble like the rest of us."

"That's because she's a child," Walid replied, pressing a hand to his forehead before letting it drop heavily. He looked away. "Even if I wanted to leave, I can't. Aliyah's not well enough and right now she needs stability. And if it's true that Josh is out there preparing to attack...maybe we should hang back a bit."

Minnesota and Spacey exchanged glances, then looked at Mason, silent but expectant. It was clear the two of them had been having private conversations that extended beyond the group's discussions.

"He's forgetting things," Minnesota said quietly. "I noticed when we first moved down here but now it seems worse. Something is bothering him but I don't know what."

"Forgetting things?" Mason frowned. "What you talking about?"

"He's having brief memory lapses," she explained, her voice edged with concern. "Like he told us to meet up with him earlier but when we met him he looked pissed. Like he forgot."

By T. STYLES

Walid's face showed his great concern. "And today he called me Ace."

"Whoa," Spacey said.

"Well, we know he had brain surgery. Maybe it's a side effect," Mason replied, trying to rationalize something that was irrational.

"That could be true," she admitted, though her voice sounded hollow. "But... what if it's not? What if he has Alzheimer's or —"

"I don't want to hear that shit," Mason interrupted sharply. "He's not sick or anything like that. If anything, he's under a lot of stress."

His gaze hardened as he looked at each of them.

Walid, one of his two living sons touched his shoulder lightly in support.

Taking a deep breath Mason said, "But that doesn't change my mind about finding our own places on the outside. I'm gonna look into a few options. But there's this new development I know about, a friend of mine owns it. It's a luxury high-rise, and he hasn't put the units on the market yet. So it's way under the radar. No listings, no official address."

"Which means he can't find us," Minnesota added.

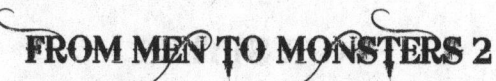

Spacey nodded thoughtfully. "That sounds good. But when will they be ready?"

"A week from now," Mason replied.

Walid shook his head slowly. "I want you all to be safe if you really think there's an issue with father. But I won't lie, this is hard. Because…if it's true that he's sick — "

"He's not," Mason cut in, voice firm.

"But if it is true," Walid continued, "Doesn't he need us? And if you go, that also leaves me with him at a time when I'm not sure how to handle it alone. I got Aliyah. And the boys." He paused, glancing around the room. "And have we all forgotten about Joey? Do we leave him and Quinn to figure things out on their own? We may not be a great family, but we still family. I'm not saying you shouldn't go through with your plans. I'm just saying…be sure before you make any moves."

They all fell silent, each lost in thought, the weight of Walid's words settling over them.

After a moment, Walid spoke again, his voice steady. "Since we know a week is the deadline, let's start paying closer attention to him. Spend more time with him."

"You mean really observe his ass, huh, little brother?" Spacey added.

"Exactly. But not only him, these people he has here. Let's see how the handlers act around us too. If, after everything, we decide he's dangerous…then, sick or not, I'll figure out what to do with Aliyah and Joey. But if we do this…" he looked around, his gaze steady, "we do it as a family."

Mason felt a swell of pride as he looked at his son. He'd always known Walid was a good man but hearing him speak with such resolve and maturity left him almost speechless.

"Alright," Mason said, nodding firmly. "We stick close to him. So close he might start suspecting, but it doesn't matter. We need to be sure."

Minnesota glanced around, her look cautious but determined. "Just so I'm clear…what exactly are we trying to be sure of?"

Mason's eyes looked at his family. "We making sure this nigga not fucking crazy."

Walid entered his room, his footsteps slowing as he took in the sight before him. Aliyah was leaning over the bed,

struggling to pack clothes into a large suitcase. Her movements were slow and strained, her face etched with fatigue.

He rushed to her side, gently taking hold of her shoulders. "What you doing?" He asked, concern evident in his voice.

She looked up at him. "I'm leaving, Walid. I can't stay here and be a part of… whatever is happening with your family. Especially knowing it's all my fault."

Walid shook his head, carefully helping her back onto the bed. He pulled the covers up to her breasts, tucking them around her with a tenderness born from worry and love.

"You're nowhere near responsible for any of this," he said softly. "My family always got some shit going on. And what you trying to do…set yourself back? You aren't well, baby. Plus, do you want me to be under this kind of pressure?"

"What you talking about?" She asked, a hint of defiance in her voice.

"If you leave, you'll mess everything up," he replied, steady but pleading. "There are things going on with my family, things I need to sort out. But the last thing I want is for you to do so much that now I have to worry about your

By T. STYLES

safety too. I don't wanna snap, Aliyah. Stay sturdy, baby. I need you."

He leaned down, pressing a soft kiss to her forehead, then her lips. The scent of her perfume filled him with a sense of calm he rarely felt.

"I understand, Walid. I guess I'm just being selfish."

"You're not. You just have to give things time, Aliyah. Let the situation play out. When it does, I promise you'll be safe. I'll be safe. And so will Baltimore and Roman."

He spoke their names with a fierce protectiveness. Baltimore was his 7-year-old son and Roman was his 5-year-old nephew whom he cared for. Roman was Ace's child, Walid's twin brother who had taken his own life right before Walid's eyes. The memory stung deeply, a wound that never truly healed. Caring for his nephew as if he were his own, was a promise Walid made that day, to always look out for Roman. And he intended to keep that promise.

"Please, just…sit back. I've got us," he assured her.

She met his gaze and nodded. "I will trust you, because I know I can."

This made Walid stand tall. "Do you want anything?" He asked gently. "Like tea?"

She smiled softly. "Please. With three cubes of sugar and lemon."

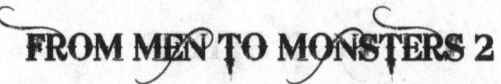

Walid nodded and turned to leave, pausing at the doorway to look back at her one last time. The sight of her resting, finally at ease, filled him with a renewed sense of purpose.

Walid intended to check on his son, Baltimore, and his nephew, Roman, but first he made a detour to the kitchen to prepare Aliyah's tea, as she had requested. The more rested she was the better so he wanted her to have what she desired. He steeped the tea leaves carefully, adding three sugar cubes and a slice of lemon.

After bringing the tea into their room, he set off to check on the boys.

As he opened their bedroom door, an unexpected scent hit him.

The distinct smell of smoke.

Frowning, he stepped inside, his eyes scanning the room. There, he saw a faint white puff of smoke rising from in front of the boys, who had their backs turned to him. The smoke curled from the side of the bed, just out of his view.

"What's going on?" Walid demanded, his voice tight with concern. He put the flames out with a pillow and then rushed to add water in the bathroom. When he was done he faced the boys. "Fuck is y'all doing?"

Roman shot up, startled, and turned to face his uncle. "I'm sorry, uncle," he stammered. "I just...wanted to see if the fire could grow."

"What you mean you wanted to see if the fire could grow?" Walid's voice was sharp, his gaze fixed intently on the boy. Roman although young was starting to be just like his evil father.

"I mean...I wanted to see if the fire could get...high," Roman said, his explanation almost casual.

A surge of rage coursed through Walid. Recently, incidents like this had become disturbingly common whenever the boys were together, and it pained him to think that Roman might be turning out like Ace.

A path that spelled nothing but danger for their family.

"You can't be in here burning shit," Walid said, his voice stern as he stepped forward and gripped Roman's arm. He applied just enough pressure to make his point. "This house is below ground. One small fire here could kill everyone inside, and no one would ever find us. Are we clear?"

Roman looked up, eyes wide, and nodded softly. "Yes, uncle."

"Don't hurt him, father," Baltimore interjected, stepping in protectively. "He understands now. Right, Roman?"

Roman nodded again, glancing from Baltimore to Walid. "I understand."

Walid released his grip, his voice softening slightly. "Good. Now, go to the kitchen. Anna's made you both sandwiches."

"Yes, father," Baltimore replied obediently, hugging his legs before leaving.

"Yes, uncle," Roman added, his voice subdued. "I'm sorry again. I really am."

Walid watched as the boys filed out of the room, their heads lowered. He waited until they were out of sight before letting out a long, heavy sigh. Consumed with agitation, he walked over to Baltimore's bed and sat down heavily on the edge, pressing both hands to his face as if to wipe away the frustration building within him.

With everything spiraling out of control around him, this was the last thing he needed.

And yet here he was.

CHAPTER EIGHT

Josh Fisher sat in the far corner of a public library, deeply absorbed in *The Art of War*. Though he owned several copies, something about reading it here, surrounded by shelves brimming with stories, knowledge, and unspoken power, made the words resonate more. The quiet of the library seemed to amplify each phrase, allowing them to seep into his bones.

For a while, he felt at home in the silence, until he noticed two familiar men approach. Both wore black slacks and black shirts. Their brown skin seemed to glow under the soft library lights. They waited patiently as Josh finished the final sentence, his finger tracing each word slowly before he closed the book.

"What you find out?" Josh asked, his voice low and controlled.

"This is a very powerful family," the man with a gray beard replied, his tone laced with caution. "I think you should be careful about how we move."

Josh leaned back, crossing his arms over his chest, the slight rustle of his shirt breaking the silence. He stroked his chin thoughtfully, feeling the warmth of his skin as he considered the man's words.

"How wealthy are you?" Josh asked, his voice almost mocking.

Gray Beard hesitated, glancing toward the man on his right, who was bald and stood silent. "Not very," he admitted finally.

Josh nodded, his expression unchanged. "Then answer me this...who comes to you for what you think, and then pays you for it?"

Gray Beard sighed, clearly catching on. "No one."

"Exactly," Josh said, a sharp edge in his voice. He took a deep breath, his frustration held just beneath the surface. "I need to find her." A stiff finger pointed into the cool table. "Now." He sat deeper into the chair. "Now I know she had something to say about being with Walid and—."

"Not just something to say," Bald Head interjected quietly. "But the woman made it clear, with her own voice, that she chose him. And as far as I know, that was your requirement."

Josh clenched his fists, his anger barely restrained. "Yes, she did tell me she chose him. But I also remember the stories she told me about him, about how dangerous he was. About his father and his "pops" too. So," he continued, his eyes narrowing, "if I look into her eyes and she tells me she

By T. STYLES

doesn't want me, then all of this will end. But if I see even a glimmer of hope, I'm taking her with me, willingly or not."

The two men exchanged a tense glance, understanding the determination in his voice. He was in the type of love that got niggas killed or started wars.

Without another word, Josh reopened his book, his fingers sliding over the well-worn pages. He began to read passages he practically knew by heart. The faint scent of aged paper filled the air as he immersed himself once more in his familiar study.

"Go find her," he whispered without looking up. "And get the gangs involved if you have to. I've done a lot to keep them out of prison. They owe me this."

The men nodded silently and walked away, leaving Josh alone in the quiet sanctity of the library.

The handlers hung in the hallways and throughout the house like black bats. Serving no real purpose but still being in the way.

Hovering.

Watching.

At the end of the day they were getting on everybody's fucking nerve. Even Sugar stepped on one of their toes because he kept following her.

The only one who didn't have a problem was Banks.

He sat lounged in the dimly lit room, a thick haze of smoke curling around him as he held a cigar between his fingers, savoring the earthy aroma mixed with hints of leather and cedar. The cigar's tip smoldered a warm red, casting a soft glow that flickered in time with his slow, measured puffs.

The door opened, and Mason stepped in, taking in the rich scent filling the air. "I was just about to light one myself," he said, crossing the room.

Banks nodded, gesturing with the cigar. "What's stopping you?"

Mason took his own cigar, carefully cutting the tip with practiced precision. He struck a gold lighter, causing the tip to burn orange.

"Do you remember when we first met?" Mason asked, his vision briefly obscured by the swirl of smoke that drifted between them as he took a seat.

Banks raised an eyebrow, exhaling another stream of smoke. "Why do I feel like this is a setup?"

"Do you remember?" Mason's voice held a note of insistence.

"I remember plenty of shit," Banks replied coolly. "For instance...how you helped me when I needed you most, back when we were growing up. And how I returned the favor, many, many times over since then. I even made you and your family independently wealthy for life," he continued, his tone sharpening. "I've always put you first, Mason, and yet here I am...having my loyalty repaid with doubt and mistrust."

Mason watched him carefully, searching for something in Banks' words, a subtle clue to gauge the state of his friend's memory. But he could see this conversation was veering somewhere else entirely...toward barely concealed resentment.

But Mason wouldn't be baited. He took a long draw on his cigar, his mind steady.

"Do you remember hanging on the block?" Mason asked quietly. "All the stories we shared in Baltimore?"

Banks narrowed his eyes. "Where you going with this, Mason?"

"I'm just asking a simple question," Mason replied, setting his cigar down in the glass ashtray beside him. "I don't see why it's causing so much strife."

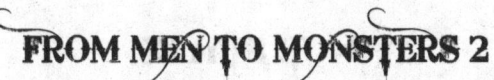

Banks leaned forward, his eyes piercing. "Do you know why this makes me uncomfortable?"

"I'm listening, brother," Mason said, his voice calm.

"Because I don't trust your ass," The bitterness evident in his statement. "I don't trust nothing about you no more."

Mason leaned back, absorbing the harshness of the words. Yet in some strange way, Banks' honesty reassured him. The man before him was still Banks, no matter how severe his accusations sounded. Maybe he wasn't losing memory, but instead was losing reason.

"I don't know what you want from me, Banks," Mason said quietly. "If there's something you think you know...then just say it."

"Not right now," Banks answered, a hint of vulnerability in his voice.

"Why not?" Mason pressed, searching his friend's face.

"Because I don't think I could handle it," Banks admitted, his gaze fixed on the cigar in his hand. "I expect my kids to be ungrateful. I expect Zoa to defy me. But you? You've been here since the beginning, Mason. Lately, it feels like you care about everyone...but me."

"Never," Mason interrupted, his voice rising in protest. "Never."

Banks laughed.

Mason's jaw clenched as he searched for the right words, the weight of the unspoken between them pressing down. "I would do anything for you," he said finally, his voice firm.

"Then prove it. Be on my side through all of this." He took a long, deep breath, the smoke drifting from his mouth as he continued. "Because I can feel them tearing apart everything I'm trying to build."

"And what exactly is that?" Mason asked, his inquisition challenging.

"Obedience," Banks answered, the conviction in his voice tinged with desperation.

Mason shook his head, leaning forward. "You can't force people to obey you, Banks. If you want loyalty, you have to start by being loyal yourself."

With that, Mason pressed the cigar into the ashtray, extinguishing it with a final twist before standing. Without another word, he turned and walked out.

Banks sat alone, staring at the smoldering tip of his cigar. His mind raced, resentment boiling over. They all judged him, pointing fingers without knowing the weight he carried.

The sacrifices he made.

If they didn't fall in line soon, they'd see just how far he was willing to go.

Spacey stood in the kitchen, carefully slicing a sandwich in half. The smell of toasted bread and melted cheese filled the air. He had made the sandwich as a gesture, hoping to share a quiet moment with Banks and speak openly about the concerns that weighed on him. The objective was clear, just as it was for Minnesota, Walid, and Mason.

To see if his father was well.

But as Spacey turned around, a foul odor hit him, cutting through the warmth of the kitchen like a cold slap. He looked up, his eyes falling on Lorna, who stood by the doorway, watching him.

Lorna was striking, her appearance floppy, with features that could pass as either Black or white. Yet there was something unsettling about her, amplified by the sharp, sour smell lingering around her.

"You really should bathe more often," he said, his voice low, but his tone unmistakable. "If you expect us to follow

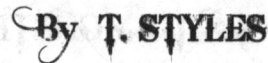

your lead and smell your pussy too...well that's just unfair."

Lorna chuckled, a single, humorless sound. "What are you doing?"

Spacey frowned, his eyes narrowing. "Mommy is that you?"

"Don't make me repeat myself," she replied, her voice turning icy. "I want to know what's going on with you. What are you up to?"

Spacey crossed his arms over his chest, meeting her gaze defiantly. "You feel real comfortable stepping up to me when you shouldn't. And I don't like that about you."

She tilted her head, smiling as she reached out, her fingers brushing the side of his face. Her palm was surprisingly soft.

"When I was growing up in South Africa," she began, her voice dripping with false sweetness, "there was a small town of beautiful men who looked just like you. There would be an auction, and the highest bidder could buy you, to do with as they pleased."

A cold wave of nausea washed over Spacey, his stomach twisting at her words. "Are you threatening to have me raped?" He asked, his voice laced with anger and disgust.

She leaned in, her smile widening. "Let me make myself clear," she whispered. "You either fall in line, or you fall down. Because you might not believe me, but I'm trying to keep you safe. To keep you well."

Spacey clenched his jaw, feeling a surge of rage building within him. "You don't know nothing about me or my family," he shot back. "So if you could just step the fuck out the way, that would be better."

"I will get from you what Banks desires."

"And you'll do that by killing us?" He said, his words tinged with dark humor at the horrific thought.

She shrugged nonchalantly. "I believe you think this sandwich will be for your father. But I want you to leave him be. He's expecting company. Talk to him later."

"You not gonna keep me from my own people. You know that, right?"

Lorna's only response was to reach out, grab half of the sandwich he had so carefully prepared, and walk away, leaving the foul odor lingering in her wake.

Spacey watched her go, fury boiling just beneath his surface.

Zoa entered the living room flanked by two handlers, one on either side of her. Her long, beautiful locs cascaded down her back, framing her chocolate face in waves of rich, dark curls that stopped just at her waist. As the men removed the black blindfold, she found herself staring directly into Banks Wales' intense gaze.

She sighed, exasperated. "Is this how it's going to be from now on? I have to be summoned instead of visiting you like an adult?"

Banks reached out, taking her hand gently. Without responding, he led her over to the bar, not bothering to ask what she wanted. He pulled a chilled glass from the small refrigerator beneath the counter, pouring a classic White Russian...a smooth blend of Kahlúa, vodka, and Baileys. The aroma of the coffee liqueur filled the space as he handed her the drink and guided her to the sofa, where they sat side by side.

Banks leaned closer, brushing her hair back from her face, his fingers lingering as he looked into her eyes. "What are you doing here?"

She let out a soft laugh, but the humor quickly faded. "What do you mean, what am I doing here? You brought me here, didn't you?"

Banks raised an eyebrow, a faint smirk playing at his lips. "You didn't tell me you were coming, Zoa."

She gave him a skeptical look. "Banks, if I hadn't told you, then why was I blindfolded? I don't even know where you live. Lately it's always with the blindfolds. So yes, you had to have told me to come here. Now are you okay?"

He chuckled, though there was an edge to it. "I'm just messing with you. Of course I sent for you."

Zoa narrowed her eyes, sensing something was off, but she didn't press him. She missed him and was happy to see his face. So, she reached out, wrapping her hands around his, pulling them into her lap. "I've missed you so much. It feels like forever since the last time I saw you. How is everything going with the family? I didn't see anyone on my way inside, but with the men you sent for me, I have a feeling…things aren't well."

Banks pulled his hands away from hers, his expression hardening. She used the nervous moment to take a sip from her glass.

"My family is my family," he said curtly. "And you know how I feel about that."

"I do," she replied softly. "I just want the best for—"

"Let me stop you right there." His voice was sharp. "You won't take my ring. You won't even consider being my wife, yet you feel it's your place to involve yourself in family matters?"

She set her glass down, her brow creasing. "Banks, that's not what I meant."

"Then what do you mean?" His voice was laced with frustration.

"I feel hate in this house," she said plainly. "Pure hate. And if that doesn't change, I don't want a front seat for it anymore."

"And you don't want to be with me either. I'm correct right?"

She looked him straight in the eyes. "I can't be with you the way you want. You want a woman who does as she's told, without thought or feeling. From the moment we met all those years ago, I admired that strength in you. But when you left me without warning, when you moved out of the country…I nearly didn't recover."

"I've heard this story before and I'm tired of it," he replied dismissively.

"And you'll hear it again anyway. And again, until it finally sinks in." She grabbed his hand. "I don't need you to rescue me, Banks. I need a companion. And if that's not something you can give me...then I'm sorry. For both of us."

She picked up her purse and rose to her feet. But as she moved toward the door, the men who had escorted her in suddenly stepped into her path. This was no polite pause to see if she needed anything; they stood like guards, blocking her exit, a silent, barrier.

Zoa glanced down at Banks, her eyes flashing with anger and hurt. "Are you going to tell them to let me leave?"

Banks remained silent, his face hardening, rage simmering.

"Banks!" She repeated, her voice firmer, more demanding. "Are you going to tell them to let me leave?"

He looked at her, a dark expression crossing his face. "I'm tired of trying to catch a slippery fish, Zoa. One day, you're going to jump into my pan or die a painful death."

"Die a painful...."

At his nod, the men quickly stepped forward, slamming the blindfold over her eyes again, but this time with rough hands and none of the earlier care. The last thing she felt was a jarring tug as they guided her out of the room.

By T. STYLES

Zoa stood on a gravel road, the rough stones pressing beneath her feet as she held her breath, waiting for the car behind her to pull away. Blindfolded, she listened as the engine revved and the tires crunched over the gravel, the sound fading into the distance until silence settled around her. Only then did she remove the blindfold.

Still afraid, she found herself next to her car, her heart still pounding. Quickly, she slid into the driver's seat, her hands trembling as she gripped the steering wheel. Fear clawed at her so intensely that her fingers kept slipping off the start button as she tried to get the engine running. She took a shaky breath, attempting to calm herself, when suddenly, the passenger-side door opened.

A man eased smoothly into the seat beside her. He was beautiful, with deep chocolate skin that caught the late afternoon light. For a brief, horrified moment, Zoa froze, yet something about his calm demeanor reassured her. Oddly, she realized she felt less afraid now than she had moments earlier with Banks, the man she once believed she loved.

"Who are you?" She asked, voice barely more than a whisper.

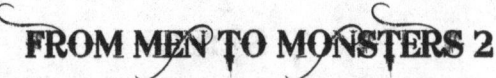

"My name is Josh Fisher," he replied, his tone calm and steady. "I'm a friend of Aliyah."

"Aliyah?" Zoa echoed, her voice filled with surprise and suspicion.

Josh leaned forward, his eyes meeting hers with intensity. "Let's just say...I'm concerned for her safety and well-being."

"Aliyah?" Zoa's voice softened, a trace of protectiveness surfacing. "Walid would never hurt her."

Josh shook his head, his expression somber. "I'm not talking about Walid. I'm talking about Banks."

The name sent a chill through her, and after the day's events, she believed him without hesitation.

"Can we go somewhere and talk alone?" Josh asked.

Zoa's gaze drifted to her driver's side window, where she noticed two men standing watch. In her rearview mirror, she saw three more positioned strategically behind her car.

"Are you going to...human traffic me or something?" She asked, a forced attempt at humor masking her genuine fear.

"Never," Josh replied sincerely. "I only want to help Aliyah." He took a deep breath. "May I reach into my pocket? I'm asking so I don't alarm you."

Zoa nodded slowly, her eyes trained on him, her mind cautious but intrigued. He pulled out his phone and handed it to her.

"What is this for?" She asked, glancing down at the screen.

"Look," he replied.

She scrolled through the images, photo after photo of Josh and Aliyah together. In every picture, Aliyah's smile was radiant, her eyes bright with happiness. Zoa couldn't help but smile herself, feeling a flicker of warmth, though it quickly darkened as her mind returned to the gravity of the situation.

She handed the phone back to him. "Alright. Let's talk."

CHAPTER NINE

Quinn had just finished getting Joey ready for bed, making sure he was clean and comfortable beneath the covers. She turned off the main light, leaving only the soft glow of a lamp in the far corner, casting a gentle warmth across the room. Settling into a nearby chair, she opened her book, savoring the quiet, when the door creaked open.

Immediately, a pungent odor filled the space, thick and sour, turning her stomach. Quinn glanced up, bracing herself.

"Joey is asleep," she said, her voice polite but firm. "Is there something I can help you with?"

Lorna stepped further into the room, her presence making the smell even stronger.

"Lorna," Quinn repeated, her tone growing more insistent. "Is there something I can help you with?"

But Lorna didn't answer. Instead, with her arms clasped tightly behind her back, she tilted her head, casting her surveillance over Joey's peaceful face as if studying him. Truth be told she wished she'd get the fuck out because the stench was driving her insane.

"I happened to see some videos of him back when he could walk. He was a very handsome young man, don't you think?"

"He's handsome now."

"That he is…"

Quinn felt a flicker of unease but kept her temper steady. "If there's something you need, please let me know."

Lorna's eyes remained on Joey, her gaze oddly intense. "If only they knew how good they have it," she murmured.

"What do you mean?" Quinn asked, her patience thinning.

"The Wales and Louisville families. I mean even with him disabled, probably for the rest of his life, he lives in luxury," Lorna replied, finally shifting her focus to Quinn. "Even his classically beautiful white housemaid cares enough to stay by his side when she should be off duty."

Quinn sighed, understanding the insinuation. "I've been watching after Joey beyond my scheduled hours since I started this job. I usually wait until he's deeply asleep before leaving."

Lorna's glare narrowed suspiciously. "So tell me something, why do you do that?"

"Because he often wakes up in pain. Some nights are easier for him, but others… let's just say he needs someone close by." She paused, meeting Lorna's eyes. "But where are you going with this?"

"Are you familiar with Josh?"

"Of course not."

"So how do you know the name?"

"I didn't attend the meeting but Joey gave me a brief later."

"Mmmm….hmmmm." Lorna straightened, her posture stiff, her demeanor laced with warning. "I am his point person…his handler. It's my responsibility to ensure he has everything he needs." Her voice hardened. "Do you understand where I'm going with this?"

Quinn's jaw tightened. "I would never hurt Joey."

"Oh, I know you wouldn't," Lorna replied, suddenly cold, threatening. "You're not that stupid."

Quinn clenched her hands, forcing herself to remain calm. "I understand that you have responsibilities, but there's no reason to be unpleasant about it."

Lorna laughed, though it held no warmth. She cocked her head, a mocking smile on her face. "I say what I mean."

"And I do too. So let me say this…you should really consider bathing more often than once a month," Quinn added, unable to hold back. "I mean, what on earth are you eating to smell this bad? It's one thing not to bathe, but you smell like—"

"Careful," Lorna interrupted, her finger pointed threateningly in Quinn's direction. "Be very careful what you say next."

She turned her gaze back to Joey, studying him as if considering something sinister. "I'll allow you to stick around after hours...for now. But if I even suspect you mean harm to a single hair or limb on his body," she said, her voice low and menacing, "you'll be dealing with me."

Walid had just finished tucking the boys into bed and making sure Aliyah was settled before deciding to visit his father. As he moved through the quiet hallway, an unpleasant odor hit him before he even saw her. He paused, glancing down for a moment, bracing himself, and then looked up to meet her eyeline.

"What do you want?" He asked firmly, leaving little room for nonsense.

Lorna stood there, hands clasped tightly behind her back, a smug smile on her face. "I was going to ask you the same thing."

Walid narrowed his eyes, his patience thinning. "I'm going to see my father."

"He's not accepting visitors right now," she replied, her voice edged with authority.

"I'm confused about exactly what it is you do here." If her role was truly to protect the family, then in his mind, that meant she worked for him, not the other way around.

"I am here to make sure you're safe," she said, her tone condescending. "Banks told you already."

He stepped closer, ignoring the foul smell emanating from her. "Well, you should take care to make sure you're safe too. Sometimes people get so wrapped up in other people's wellbeing, that they forget to look after their own."

"Are you threatening me?"

"Yes," he replied without hesitation, moving even closer, his glare unwavering. "Yes, I am. I don't like you. I don't like your energy. I don't like what you represent." His voice grew colder. "I don't like how you smell, and I certainly don't like the authority you think you have over my family."

The smug smile disappeared from her face.

 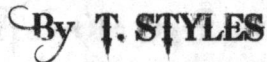

"I don't know where he found you," Walid continued, his voice low and resolute, "but I intend on finding out and sending you back."

She clenched her jaw.

"I'll come back later," he said, "But let me be clear…this will be the last time you stop me from seeing my flesh and blood."

Walid held her gaze, letting the tension hang between them.

Then, with a final, deliberate look that traveled from her eyes down to her feet and back, he turned on his heel, leaving her standing there, stunned and seething.

Minnesota paced the length of her bedroom, her heart racing as she repeatedly glanced at the door. At last, it opened, and Mason, Walid, and Spacey entered. Walid closed the door firmly behind him, turning the lock with a click that seemed to settle Minnesota, if only slightly.

"What's wrong, big sis?" Walid asked, studying her with concern.

"We have to find out who that woman is," Minnesota said, her voice laced with urgency. "Do you know I went to check on Sugar, and she was holding her? Just…picked her up for no fucking reason! Talking about Banks wanted her to check on his baby!"

"Ew!" Spacey grimaced. "That skunk touched our bloodline?"

"Exactly," Minnesota replied, her face twisting with disgust. "Sugar's clothes smelled so bad; I burned them in the incinerator."

"What's up with this creep?" Spacey asked. "I had a run-in with her too. I was making a sandwich for pops when she took half of it and told me I couldn't see him."

"She blocked me too," Walid added, crossing his arms as the irritation settled into his expression. "But it won't happen again."

They all looked toward Mason.

"I haven't run into her yet," he said, "but that doesn't mean I won't."

Walid exhaled, nodding thoughtfully. "Since we can't see how father is doing, maybe I'm wrong about how we should approach this."

"What you mean?" Spacey said.

"The objective was to gauge his mood but she's always around. So we do need a plan." Walid sighed deeply. "At the same time, this is gonna sound crazy, but I don't feel comfortable leaving father alone with her."

"Me either," Spacey agreed.

"I don't feel well about it myself," Minnesota added.

"Pops, do you have any idea where she came from?" Walid asked, looking to Mason for answers.

Mason let out a deep sigh and sank into the soft yellow recliner in the corner of Minnesota's spacious room, his look distant as he gathered his thoughts. "I have an idea."

"Where?" Walid pressed, moving closer.

"She probably belongs to this…church that we used to go to," he explained slowly.

Spacey's eyebrows shot up. "Y'all were involved in church? But everybody in this house heathens."

"First of all we not heathens. We believe in the Lord. But not following him may be why we fucked up right now."

Everyone felt it was just the old settling in because Mason never spoke like this.

"Like I was saying, we were involved in church, but it wasn't a typical church," he continued. "It had a Catholic feel but was anything but. They had some very strict beliefs, especially about…certain people." His voice trailed off, the implication clear.

"Certain people?" Spacey asked. "Gays? Straights?"

"Nah…anybody who didn't pay them." Mason said. "It was more about control and money. And when those beliefs became too extreme, he stopped going. I stopped with him. We were way young. Only had Spacey I think."

"So what happened? Why he stop?"

"They wanted him to give them everything. Money. Control. And even Spacey."

They all glanced at one another, a grim understanding settling in.

"The firstborn?" Walid said.

"Yep…to raise him in the church. But a lot of shit popped off and he didn't go that way. But to this day I wonder if he considered it."

"If its them, why would he allow them to help him now?" Minnesota asked, shaking her head in disbelief.

Mason's eyes darkened with contemplation. "My theory is…he's feeling guilt. Rage. I don't all the way know."

Walid took a deep breath, the realization dawning on him. "I know why," he said, his voice almost a whisper. "He may be losing it."

All eyes turned to him, and he took on the weight of their attention.

"He's feeling guilty about Ace," Walid said quietly. "I told y'all he called me his name. But I be trying to talk to him about it. Just to see how he's doing since he pressed so hard for him to be killed. But he says fuck that nigga. I know that's not what's pumping through his heart though."

A collective sigh filled the room as understanding washed over them.

"Sounds about right. Because despite what he says," Mason continued, "Banks acts like he's fine with how everything went down with Ace...but it's eating at him. And what's worse, he's unwilling to talk about it."

"So, he punishes himself by turning to this strange religious cult?" Minnesota asked.

"And he hates us for not letting Ace go," Spacey added.

"I guess it's what he thinks he needs right now," Mason replied.

"I'm scared," Minnesota admitted, her voice trembling. "Like really fucking scared."

Walid moved to her side, wrapping an arm around her shoulders. "We gonna protect you," he promised softly.

"You know that, right?" Spacey added, his face serious. She nodded, feeling the comfort of their presence.

"Let's get confirmation about this woman first," Walid said, looking at Mason. "Can you find out if she's really connected to this group, pops?"

"Yeah, I'll work on it," Mason replied with a firm nod. "I think we should also keep looking into places of our own," he continued. "If these people are as dangerous as we suspect, this won't end well. A Whale, like Banks, only comes once in a lifetime. So letting him go may not end without a fight."

By T. STYLES

CHAPTER TEN

Zoa sat across from Josh in an elegant restaurant, its dim lighting casting a warm glow over their table. She took in his handsome features, the strong lines of his jaw and the way his eyes seemed to hold a depth she hadn't expected. Although the setting felt intimate, she reminded herself of the real purpose of their meeting. This was far from a romantic evening.

"Where are you from?" Josh asked, his voice soft yet probing.

She tilted her head, giving him a curious look. "You don't have to do that with me," she said very direct. "Just come out and tell me what it is you want."

He chuckled, leaning back in his chair, his legs crossing as he relaxed, his hands resting loosely on his lap. "We'll get to that," he replied. "Are you in a rush?"

She let out a sigh, her glare sharp. "I'd just prefer to know what you want with me."

"Alright, let's do this," he said, glancing down at his watch. "In exactly five minutes, I'll tell you what it is I want, as long as you allow me those five minutes to just get to know you. Besides, we might find ourselves in a situation where we really need one another. Deal?"

She couldn't help but smile, caught off guard by his charm, though she hated how easily he disarmed her. "Deal," she replied, leaning back. "Five minutes." She smiled. "I'm from Ghana."

His face lit up in surprise. "You're kidding."

"I don't joke about my heritage or my country," she said, her voice carrying a note of pride.

"Before I tell you why that makes me smile, let me show you something." He reached into his pocket, pulling out his phone. After a few taps, he handed it to her.

She looked down to see a photo of him dressed in traditional Ghanaian attire, rich with vibrant colors and intricate patterns. Her mouth fell open slightly.

"You're from Ghana too," she said, handing back his phone with a hint of newfound warmth.

"I wanted you to see that I'm not a liar," he replied, slipping the cell back into his pocket.

"I don't know you well enough to call you a liar. But I appreciate you showing me all the same."

Josh nodded, his expression contemplative. "Yes, I've lived here most of my life, but my parents made sure I returned to Ghana regularly. So I can know where I'm from, to be sure where I'm going. But how often do you go back, Zoa?"

"I was just there," she admitted, then looked away, her mood suddenly shifting.

He leaned forward, concern crossing his face. "Are you alright?" He asked, reaching across the table to touch her hand gently.

She pulled back, slowly, hesitantly. "I'm fine. It's just that, I had to come back because…something was going on with Banks," she said, her voice barely above a whisper.

Josh sighed. "If I believe Aliyah, and I assure you I do, there always seems to be something going on with that man. And the Wales family."

"You seem to know a lot about him," she remarked, eyeing him suspiciously.

He leaned back, his gaze fixed. "As I said, Aliyah and I are friends. I probably know more about Banks than you do."

"Like what?"

"The people he's hurt, the things he does under the guise of 'protecting' those under his control. He is anything but a gentleman."

She held his stare, a slight challenge in her eyes. "I don't believe you."

He raised an eyebrow. "I thought we just agreed to trust each other. I told you…I don't lie."

She took a deep breath. "Then what do you want from me?"

"I want you to tell me where she is," he said simply.

Zoa shook her head. "As I told you, she's with Walid now."

He lifted his hands in a gesture of reassurance, palms open. "I don't want to take her from him. I just need her to look me in the eyes and tell me she's okay. If she does that, I'm done." He paused, his expression turning serious. "Because before I was in a relationship with her, I was her attorney."

"An attorney?" Zoa's brows knitted in surprise.

"Yes," he nodded. "I thought I mentioned that already. She was looking for a way to leave him and take Baltimore with her."

"I don't think you leave the Wales family when you want," she said.

"Maybe you do know more about him than I think you do." He said. "At first, I knew only a little about the family, but as I dug deeper after she was taken, I realized they were far more dangerous than I ever imagined."

She studied him, his words sinking in. "This is making me uncomfortable."

His eyes held a fierce urgency. "You should be. Because wherever this family goes, destruction follows. Their son, Ace I believe, was once in a boy's home, and right after they took him out, that place burned to the ground." He held her puzzled glance, his voice dropping to a murmur. "These are killers, Zoa. You have to believe me. So tell me, where does he live?"

She exhaled, looking away. "I don't know where. Whenever I go, they blindfold me."

Josh nodded, as though he'd expected this. "I understand. But this is what I'm asking as one Ghanaian to another," he said, his voice soft yet insistent. "Meet with him again. Go to the house and see if you can find any clues. A note, an address, anything that might indicate where they are."

"Why should I do that?"

"Because if you were in trouble, wouldn't you want someone to do the same for you?"

CHAPTER ELEVEN

Banks sat alone at a lavishly set breakfast table, laden with every breakfast item imaginable. Plates of fluffy scrambled eggs, crispy bacon, golden waffles, fresh fruit, and pastries surrounded him, yet the table felt hollow. He had waited fifteen minutes, hoping his family would join him, but as he looked around, he realized he was, once again, eating alone.

Sighing, he began to butter a slice of toast, spreading on more butter than necessary, each stroke a sign of his growing frustration. They were all so fucking ungrateful, he thought. Ungrateful for what he did to keep them safe, for the sacrifices he made, and the responsibilities he shouldered. The bitterness settled in his chest, heavy and exhausting.

Suddenly, Mason walked in, the aroma of coffee and warm bread greeting him.

"Are you gonna eat all of this yourself?" Mason joked, trying to lighten the mood.

But Banks didn't return the friendly gesture, keeping his stare fixed on his toast. Mason shrugged and sat down beside him, pouring himself a cup of coffee and reaching for a croissant.

"So you didn't work on the family like I asked you to. This is how they repay me? With disrespect! And not coming to breakfast!"

"I don't wanna play games with you anymore," Mason said, his tone serious. "Niggas don't fuck with you right now."

"So you admit you have been gaming. And they have too." Banks chuckled. "Well, there's something we can agree on."

Mason took a deep breath. "Are those people...Lorna and the handlers you got watching us...are they from that church? *The Bells Of The Chosen Disciples*."

Banks' eyes moved to Mason before returning to his toast, where he smeared another dollop of butter.

"Banks, are they with *The Bells Of The Chosen Disciples*?" Mason pressed.

"You sound foolish," Banks replied, his voice hard and dismissive. "Why do you say that?"

"I remember the clothing."

"Cut it out."

"So, they aren't?" Mason leaned forward, refusing to let the question drop. "This isn't some strange way to punish yourself for—"

"For what?" Banks' voice rose, cutting Mason off.

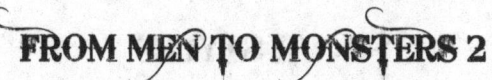

"For what happened with Ace. Because I been trying to tell you, man, that until you deal with it, it won't go away."

Banks shook his head. "Listen to you, trying to lecture me. When the truth is you didn't care anything about our son," Banks interrupted, the timber in his voice cold and accusatory. "You wanted the nigga dead just as much as I did at the end because he was dangerous. I was the only one willing to push off and I'm hated for it."

Mason's hand clenched around his coffee cup as he struggled to keep his composure. "I didn't care?" He asked, his voice low and trembling with restrained anger. "How can you say that? I was the one who begged you to make sure before we took him out. I was the one who wanted us to exhaust every other option, because I knew—"

"Knew what?" Banks roared, slamming his fist on the table, the dishes rattling from the impact.

Mason's hands shook, not from fear but from the surge of emotion that overwhelmed him. "I knew that if you didn't deal with this guilt, you'd take it out on everyone else. On your kids, on your grandkids—on this entire family. And I was right."

Banks' heart pounded in his chest, his face hardening as he glared at Mason. "You always think you know everything, but you don't. You nothing but another nigga I allowed to sit under my boot, because that's all you really good for."

Mason felt the sting of the words, a sharp pain that cut deeper than he wanted to admit. They'd been friends for so long, and no one knew how to wound him like Banks. But if it was true, that his friend was sick, wasn't he supposed to show restraint?

"If it's not about Ace is this about me? Are you crashing out because of me?"

Silence.

"Are those handlers," Mason changed the direction, his voice steady, "with *The Bells Of The Chosen Disciples*?"

Banks' eyes narrowed, his face hardening even further. "I need you to get out of my face," he said, his tone final. "I won't say it again."

Mason studied him for a moment, then stood before turning and walking away.

Mason stormed out of the kitchen, his mind racing with frustration. As he stepped into the hallway, he nearly

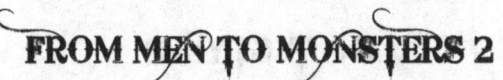

bumped into Spacey, Minnesota, and Walid, who had been waiting, their expressions tense and expectant.

"Well, what happened?" Minnesota asked.

Mason took a deep breath, glancing between them. "He won't fucking tell me," he replied, the irritation clear in his voice. "But I have an idea."

The others exchanged glances, disappointment mingling with their worry. Before they could ask more, Mason continued. "In the meantime, go meet with the person I told you about. He's going to show you some options, and then he'll send the available units to your phone. If you like them, arrange for a wire transfer before they go on the market."

"But how are we supposed to keep the handlers away?" Spacey asked, his voice edged with frustration. "They're everywhere."

"They're handlers, not eavesdroppers," Mason replied sharply. "Figure out a way to keep them the hell out of your business. Because right now, I can't think of every fucking thing."

With that, he stormed down the hallway.

"So ain't no adults left in this bitch huh?" Spacey said.

Walid and Minnesota walked away.

CHAPTER TWELVE

When Banks left the kitchen, Spacey grabbed a quick breakfast. He was making his way down the hallway when, without warning, his legs slipped out from under him. Suddenly he crashed onto his back, the impact reverberating painfully as his head hit the hard floor. A sharp cry of agony escaped him, echoing down the corridor.

Moments later, Minnesota came rushing down, her face filled with worry. "What happened? How you hurt yourself?" She was about to move closer when her foot slid slightly. Luckily she was able to catch her bearings when she looked down and noticed a slick, oily substance coating the floor.

"Why is there shit on the floor?" She shouted, glancing toward the end of the hallway.

"What shit?" He said.

"Oil. Grease! I don't fucking know."

Suddenly she saw Roman and Baltimore. Roman's face turned pale, and he quickly stammered out an apology as he held the olive oil in his hand.

He placed it down and walked toward them, with Baltimore following. "I'm so sorry, I'm so sorry!" Roman exclaimed, wringing his hands nervously. "I didn't think anyone would get hurt..."

Minnesota's eyes blazed with frustration. "Why wouldn't you think someone would get hurt?" She snapped. "You poured oil on the floor!"

"I'm sorry...I'm so sorry."

"I'm tired of you always causing trouble around here. Hurting people isn't something we do in this family." She said this despite Banks hiring what she felt were killers to watch their every move.

To the contrary, hurting people is exactly what the Wales did best.

Spacey continued to moan in pain, his gaze flickering over to the boys.

"He didn't mean it," Baltimore muttered, his voice barely audible. "Can we clean it up?"

"No!" Minnesota yelled, her tone leaving no room for argument. "Go to your room, now."

Roman and Baltimore shuffled away, their heads lowered, their footsteps fading into the distance. Once she was sure her nephews were safely out of sight, she turned toward the wall-mounted phone. Without hesitation, she picked up the receiver and dialed for medical assistance for

By T. STYLES

Spacey. A small team was stationed on duty during the week…rarely called upon, but this time would be different.

This time, their presence was urgently needed.

After getting help, Spacey lay in bed, still groaning from the pain but mostly relieved nothing was broken. The doctor had examined him, prescribed some medication, and assured them he'd recover soon. Once the doctor left, Spacey turned to Minnesota, his expression firm.

"I need you to go ahead without me," he said quietly, once the door was closed. "To meet the man."

"But I wanna make sure you gonna be good."

"I'll be fine. Pick a unit for us. Put yours and mine, next to each other. I don't care what floor," he continued.

"I don't want to leave you like this," she replied, hesitant.

"Please," Spacey insisted. "We have to make sure we have a backup plan before pops gets worse."

She sighed, finally nodding. "Are you sure?"

"I won't be in this bed long," he reassured her. "Just do it, okay?"

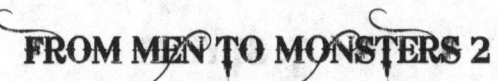

Walid had just received word that his nephew Roman was in trouble once again. Frustration simmered within him as he made his way down the hallway, his footsteps echoing softly. Behind him, the nanny, Sarah, followed, her expression calm and composed as they reached the boys' room. Walid pushed open the door with a foot.

"Fuck is wrong with you little niggas!"

Sarah jumped. "Sir, they are kids."

"Sarah, you can stand right there," he instructed, motioning for her to stay near the door. He turned his attention to Roman, who sat on the edge of the bed, looking down, guilt in his eyes.

"Roman," Walid began, his tone firm, "you are not to leave this room."

"But I'm sorry," Roman pleaded, looking up. "I didn't mean to—"

"I don't want to hear it anymore," Walid interrupted, his voice edged with frustration. "There are a lot of things happening with this family that you're too young to understand. And at the end of the day, I'm tired of trying to explain it to you. Since you wanna act like a child, you're gonna stay in this room until I say otherwise."

"Please, I don't want to," Roman whispered, his voice breaking slightly. "I'm scared to be—."

 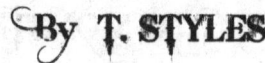 By T. STYLES

"Quiet," Walid commanded, in a harsher tone. "Sarah's going to make sure you stay put. I'm not fucking around this time."

Roman glanced over at Sarah, who gave him a solemn nod, her expression neutral but firm.

Walid continued, "Once I determine that you're ready to be responsible, then I'll consider letting you out. But not a moment before."

He looked over at his son, Baltimore, who was watching the scene with wide eyes. "Baltimore, go see about your mother. She's waiting on you."

"Yes, sir," Baltimore replied quickly, his voice obedient as he hurried out of the room.

Walid glanced back at Sarah. "You have him right?" He asked, his voice lowering slightly.

She nodded confidently. "I have him. Don't worry. He won't leave."

"Good." Walid took one last look at Roman, whose expression was now pleading.

"Uncle," Roman said softly, his voice barely more than a whisper. "Please, don't do this."

"My decision is final," he said firmly.

With that, he turned and left the room, closing the door behind him as Roman's quiet protests faded into silence.

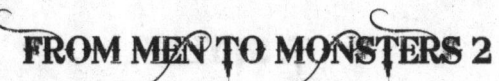

Aliyah stirred in her bed, the smooth silk of the sheets brushing against her skin. The artificial sunlight streamed in through the large window, bathing the room in a warm, golden hue. Despite its synthetic nature, it felt real enough to her. She blinked at the ceiling, her thoughts drifting to Josh.

Why hadn't he reached out?

Their friendship ended, and she knew it could go nowhere, but his silence felt unusual. The last time they spoke, he said he wouldn't believe she wanted him out of her life until he saw her face. And now, nothing. It gnawed at her. Not that she wanted him. But if it was true that he was on the enemy's list, would he apply pressure on Walid's family?

She was about to call for breakfast when the door creaked open. Her son, Baltimore, stepped inside. He moved toward her bed with a boyish eagerness, his soft footsteps barely audible on the plush carpet. Now standing beside her on the porcelain floor, he leaned in and wrapped his small arms around her.

By T. STYLES

Aliyah winced slightly, a reflex from the lingering bruises, but she let out a soft chuckle.

"I'm sorry, mommy," Baltimore said, pulling back. "I didn't mean to hurt you."

"You didn't hurt me, son," she assured him, her voice warm and soothing. "As a matter of fact, the tighter the squeeze, the better I feel." She reached out and tousled his hair.

He squeezed her again, and this time it hurt so much she shoved him hard. "That's enough honey."

"Oh...sorry, mommy."

"Where is your father?"

"Daddy's gone to take care of business," Baltimore said, his tone matter of fact.

"How are you?"

"I'm fine. Except..." He hesitated, looking down at the bedspread, his small fingers tracing invisible patterns on the fabric.

"Except what, baby?" She asked, placing a warm hand on his cheek.

"I don't understand why Roman continuously gets into trouble."

Aliyah chuckled softly, her hand now smoothing the side of his face. "Continuously?" She teased.

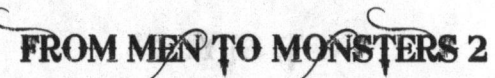

"You know what I mean, mommy," Baltimore said with a slight pout.

"Let me tell you a secret," she whispered, leaning in as if sharing a grand revelation. "When your uncle Ace was alive, he used to get into trouble too. Sometimes, that kind of mischief runs in the DNA. Maybe Roman picked up some of his ways."

Baltimore frowned. "That's not good, though. He put oil on the floor and hurt uncle Spacey."

Aliyah raised an eyebrow. "Yeah, I heard about that," she said with a sigh. "But you just stay out of trouble. Be an example, and maybe Roman will come around."

"And then he threw eggs too," Baltimore added, his face scrunching up in disapproval. "I didn't want to tell them that."

"Eggs?" Aliyah repeated, her voice tinged with disbelief.

"Yes, mommy. He threw eggs all over the house."

She let out a heavy sigh, the weight of the family's troubles pressing down on her once more. "Now that I didn't hear about," she said, shaking her head. "The last thing we need is for Roman to cause more stress. But as his cousin, you just need to be there for him. Can you do that?"

"I'll try, mommy," Baltimore said, his voice earnest.

He leaned in, kissed her hand gently, and dashed out of the room, his energy filling the air for a brief moment. The door swung slightly behind him, and Aliyah's gaze followed him as he disappeared down the hallway. A faint smile played on her lips, and she laughed softly.

"Kids will be kids," she murmured to herself.

Walid and Minnesota ascended the stairwell leading to the upper level of the house, their footsteps echoing softly against the polished wood. The upper level was a picture-perfect facade — a spacious home complete with a kitchen, nine bedrooms, and a lush backyard. Every detail was meticulously designed to appear livable, yet the truth lay below. The real home, hidden underground, was a secret fortress. Unless someone knew exactly where to enter and exit, they would never suspect the world that existed beneath their feet.

Their handlers trailed behind them, silent and watchful. As they approached the helicopter, Minnesota leaned in close to Walid, her voice low enough for only him to hear.

"I still don't see how we're going to get rid of them," she said, casting a quick glance back at the men.

Walid looked at her and smiled knowingly. "The wave."

It took her a moment, but then her face lit up with understanding. She smiled too. "Yeah, the wave."

They continued to the pad, toward the sleek black helicopter that was waiting. Its polished surface gleaming under the sunlight. Minnesota climbed in first, followed by their handlers, who took seats in the back. Walid settled into the pilot's seat, flipping switches and activating the controls. The cockpit came alive with lights and the steady whir of the rotors as they began to spin.

Before long, the helicopter lifted smoothly into the air, the ground falling away beneath them. The windows offered a panoramic view of the sprawling estate, a sight that might have felt freeing to most, but to Minnesota, it was just another reminder of the confinement they lived under.

The ride was smooth, thanks to the clear weather, but Walid couldn't resist having a little fun. With a mischievous grin, he tilted the helicopter into a steep dip and the handlers in the back lurched forward, gripping onto the sides for dear life.

By T. STYLES

Minnesota, unfazed, burst into laughter. "The wave!" She shouted gleefully, throwing her hands up in mock celebration. "Do it again!"

Walid repeated the maneuver, dipping and rising like a rollercoaster. The handlers' faces turned pale, their knuckles white as they clung to their seats. By the time they landed on Walid's rented helipad on the outskirts of D.C. the men stumbled out, their faces green and contorted with nausea. They doubled over, losing the contents of their stomachs onto the pavement.

"We're not getting back on that thing with you," one of the handlers managed to say between gasps.

"We'll meet you back at the house."

Walid smirked, leaning casually against the helicopter. "I thought y'all didn't speak," he responded, watching them stagger away.

Minnesota laughed harder, her joy infectious as Walid pulled her into a hug, squeezing her tightly. "Come on, big sis. Let's go see a nigga about a penthouse."

They made their way to the building where they were scheduled to meet a property manager. The man greeted them warmly, leading them on a tour of the units available in the complex. The penthouses were spacious and elegant and just up their rich ass alley's. By the end of the tour, they selected one for Walid and Aliyah, another for Minnesota and Sugar, and the others for Mason and Spacey. Joey would live with whoever he wanted. Each space offered enough room without anyone feeling crowded.

"I like them, just wish we could touch grass."

"These aren't permanent," Walid noted, turning to Minnesota. "Just a temporary place to regroup if things heat up." Walid sighed. "We'll take them."

The property manager shook their hands as they prepared to leave. "That's great."

"When will they be ready?"

"In about a week," the man replied. "If anything becomes available sooner, we'll let you know."

Walid and Minnesota thanked him again before heading back to their car. The ride to the helipad was quiet, the siblings were lost in thought. As they approached the helicopter, Minnesota broke the silence.

"I'm feeling good about this," she said. "I love our father, but I don't trust where he is right now."

Walid nodded. "I'm still holding onto faith that he'll be okay."

Minnesota shook her head. "You're younger than me, little brother. I've seen him at his best and worst. And trust me, where he is now…this is the lowest I've ever seen him. That means danger."

Walid and Minnesota descended the winding staircase into the dimly lit depths of Sunset Haven. When the door opened, they froze.

Banks stood on the other side, flanked by his ever-present handlers, their dark uniforms blending into the shadows. His piercing gaze locked onto them, and a thin smile played on his lips, though it held no warmth.

"I don't appreciate the little game you played," Banks said, his voice calm but angry as fuck. "Doing the wave? That was clever, I'll give you that, but let me be clear…if it happens again, Walid…" He paused, his tone turning icy. "I'll repossess your wings and you won't be flying anything, anywhere soon."

The handlers exchanged glances before breaking into low, mocking laughter, their amusement filling the space as they turned and walked away, leaving Walid and Minnesota standing alone in the weight of Banks' warning.

CHAPTER THIRTEEN

Mason gripped the steering wheel, his knuckles brushing against the smooth leather as the car hummed along the highway. Beside him, his handler sat in the passenger seat, rigid and silent. Every now and then, Mason cast a side-eyed glance at the man, his expression unreadable. It was almost comical, Mason thought, how stubbornly these guys played their roles.

Like robots.

Almost.

The air inside the car was tense as the highway stretched on, the scenery shifting from urban sprawl to sparse countryside. Mason turned off onto a quieter road, the sound of the tires crunching against gravel breaking the monotony of the drive. The trees grew denser as the car continued along the unpaved path. A quick glance at his passenger revealed the faintest shift.

The handler's head turned ever so slightly in Mason's direction.

That was enough to confirm Mason's suspicion.

He was going in the right direction.

Mason allowed himself a small smile. *Gotchu.*

The car jolted slightly as they reached a paved road again. Ahead of them, a massive structure loomed…a large new church with towering spires and new bricks. This property had gone through a renovation as Mason read the sign spelling *The Bells Of The Chosen Disciples*.

Mason slowed the car, pulling into the empty lot and the handler finally broke his silence, his voice low and laced with disdain. "You people play too many games."

Mason shifted into park, leaning back in his seat. "What do you want with my friend? What do you want with us?"

The handler smirked, his head tilting slightly as he met Mason's gaze. "I suggest you take us back to the house. Or else."

"Or else what?" Mason challenged, his voice steady, brimming with quiet authority.

The man's smirk widened, though his eyes remained cold. "You can get tough with me. But let's not forget, you've got other people you care about. People who are more vulnerable. Like Bolt and Patrick. It only takes one of them to fall to snatch some of that bravado out your chest."

Mason's jaw tightened, his grip on the steering wheel firming for a moment before he relaxed it.

"Is that what you want, old nigga?"

 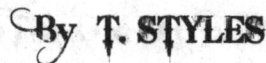

Banks sat in the center of the secret room deep within the house. The space was stark and silent, except for the faint hum of the air circulating through unseen vents. In the middle of the polished floor stood a single, imposing king's chair—black velvet with gold trimmings that glimmered faintly in the soft spotlight above. The light illuminated his figure but left the rest of the room in shadow, adding to the weight of the moment.

He wore loose white cotton pants, his chest bare, revealing intricate tattoos that stretched across his torso, each telling a story of battles fought and victories claimed. Despite his age, Banks remained fit, his body a testament to years of discipline. His gray hair framed his vanilla-colored face and highlighted his downcast eyes.

The door creaked open, cutting through the heavy silence as Lorna entered.

Her strong odor too.

"Are you ready for confession?" Lorna asked, her voice firm as she stopped before him, her arms clasped behind her back.

Banks nodded slightly, his gaze fixed on the floor.

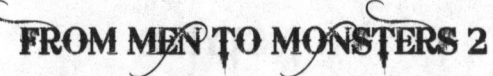

"Let me hear it," she demanded, her tone brooking no hesitation.

Banks exhaled deeply, his chest rising and falling slowly, the air heavy with the tension of unsaid words. "I hate what I've become," he said finally, his voice low, almost trembling.

"Give me more," she pressed, leaning forward ever so slightly.

Banks closed his eyes, the weight of his past pressing down on him like a vice. "I didn't know he would turn out the way he did," he began. "There was no way I could've known."

He paused, the memories threatening to consume him. The room seemed smaller now, the air thicker. "When I found out Mason...someone I thought was my best friend...had replaced his sperm with the sperm my lady and I were going to use with his own..."

"Go 'head." Lorna didn't move, her gaze steady.

Banks' voice cracked as he continued, "I knew nothing good could come from it. And yet, I held on to hope. I hoped Ace would be different. I hoped he would be like Walid."

The room felt colder.

"He wasn't."

"I need more."

 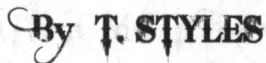

"I don't want to give more."

Lorna's voice cut through his despair like a blade. "The guilt you're feeling stems from your refusal to open up."

"I can't," Banks snapped, his head rising up to meet her eyes.

"Why?" She yelled, her voice sharp and demanding.

"Because it's not my fault!" Banks roared, his voice echoing in the room. "Yet this family blames me! Why do they blame me?!"

Lorna didn't flinch. "You were responsible for him feeling as though he needed to take his own life? Because you wanted him to be a certain person and…"

"It's not me. It's not my fault. It was him that wanted me to be something I couldn't! That I couldn't…couldn't—"

"And what was that?" Lorna asked, her tone softening ever so slightly.

Banks' voice was barely a whisper now. "His mother. He wanted me to be his mother."

The confession left him trembling, his hands gripping the arms of the chair as though they were the only things anchoring him. The pain of his words echoed in his chest, each syllable cutting deeper than the last.

"You told me they were monsters. Selfish. Greedy and capable of dark things," she said. "Is it true?"

"You don't believe me?" He responded.

"I just want to make sure."

"It is true. And if I have to relinquish my family to God to prevent something like what happened to Ace from happening to them, then so be it," Banks said finally, his voice hollow.

Lorna studied him for a moment before speaking. "Well if you want order, we're going to have to be more forceful with them," she said, her words deliberate. "Otherwise, you'll lose another child. Is that what you want?"

"You know it's not," he replied, his voice raw but steady.

"Then you have to be stronger with them. Just because they're adults doesn't mean they can do whatever they will. Especially if they're unstable and there are enemies out there trying to bring this family down."

"I understand," Banks said, his head dipping again.

"So tell me more about Josh. How dangerous is—."

"I don't feel like talking anymore."

"But I need to have intel on him if—."

"That's all I want to speak about for the day," he yelled.

Lorna's lips curled into a faint smile. "Well…I guess confession is over for the day. We'll reconvene tomorrow."

She stepped closer, and as if on cue, Banks raised his head slowly. Without warning, her hand swung, striking his right cheek with a loud smack. He didn't flinch, didn't react, but instead turned his head, offering her the other cheek. She slapped him again, and that sound also reverberated through the room.

When she turned to leave she stopped and paused. "I consider you to be powerful. And to be a master I intend on following. After all, you saved my church from closing and we all owe you a debt."

Banks smiled. "I love loyalty."

"I do too." She nodded once before disappearing through the door.

Lorna left the confession room with Banks' words still heavy in her ears. The man had a way of weaving his paranoia and conviction into her thoughts, leaving her questioning everything…even herself.

She moved through the quiet corridors of Sunset Haven, her heels clicked softly against the polished floor as she reached the control room.

The door was ajar, as it often was. Banks trusted her to monitor the house, to be his eyes and ears when he wasn't looking. It was a strange kind of trust, one born of manipulation and necessity, but trust, nonetheless. She hesitated for a moment before stepping inside, the soft hum of the monitors filling the small, sparsely lit room.

Sinking into the chair at the console, she ran her fingers over the keys, pulling up the live feeds and stored data. The screens blinked to life, showing various rooms and hallways of the sprawling mansion. She watched absently, her thoughts still tangled with Banks' declarations about the family.

Then something caught her eye...an audio file from the hallway near Mason's room. The timestamp was recent. Her curiosity piqued and Lorna clicked play. The faint hiss of static gave way to voices belonging to Walid, Spacey, Minnesota, and Mason.

She leaned closer to the speakers as Walid's voice filled the room.

"I want you all to be safe if you really think there's an issue with father," he said, his tone low and deliberate. *"But I won't lie, this is hard. Because… if it's true that he's sick —"*

"He's not," Mason interrupted, his voice firm, almost cold.

She fast forwarded the audio.

"We may not be a great family, but we're still family."

We're still family. She repeated to herself.

To Lorna he didn't sound like the monster Banks projected and yet she couldn't be sure. Not yet anyway.

Mason stormed into the basement mansion, his footsteps echoing off the sleek marble floors. His mind churned with anger that Banks had allowed *The Bells Of The Chosen Disciples* church to infiltrate their private sanctuary.

As he approached the lounge, Mason was struck by the eerie darkness that greeted him. The fake fireplace wasn't even activated, leaving the room cloaked in shadow. His eyes adjusted, and he spotted Banks sitting in silence, a glass in hand, the soft clink of ice breaking the stillness.

Mason reached for the dimmer switch, turning it just enough to illuminate the room with a gentle glow. It was enough to see Banks' face and what he saw made his stomach turn.

Bruises marked both sides of Banks' cheeks, dark and angry against his pale skin. The corner of his lip was slightly split, the dried blood catching the light. Mason's steps slowed, the initial rage replaced by a wave of concern.

"Banks, what the fuck is going on?" Mason asked, his voice quieter than he'd intended. "You letting these niggas whip on you and shit?"

Banks remained silent; his gaze focused on the amber liquid swirling in his glass.

"Brother, what's happening?" Mason pressed, moving closer. "Why you letting them people back in? Do I have to remind you how they treated you before, when you were searching for answers? If it's a church you want, I know two great ones. They're nonjudgmental, and they'll give you—"

"You know nothing," Banks interrupted, his voice sharp as a blade. "You know nothing about what I need or what this family needs either."

Mason's frustration boiled over. "These people are cult members," he said, louder now. "And they're greedy cult members at that! Did you fund that facility they just built?

By T. STYLES

Because last time I checked, it was falling into the firewood pile it was destined to be."

"So what if I did?" Banks' tone was icy. "I don't question you about what you do with yours."

Mason paced the room, the tension coiled tight in his chest. He wanted to yell, to scream, to shake Banks out of whatever madness had consumed him. He wanted to tell him that their family wasn't safe, that these people would lead him down a dark road again. But he hesitated. He wasn't sure if Banks, in his current state, could hear any of it.

Finally, Mason stopped and faced him. "I need you to put these people out. If you won't, I will."

Banks set his glass down with deliberate care and stood, his towering presence filling the space between them. "You will do nothing of the kind."

"Oh yes, I will," Mason shot back, his fists clenched at his sides.

Banks stepped closer, his voice low and dangerous. "No, you won't." He pulled out his phone, pressing a single button. "Do it."

Unsure what *do it* meant, the sound of locks clicking echoed through the mansion, a mechanical symphony of finality, gave him his answer. Mason's heart sank as he realized what just happened.

"Hold up," Mason said, his voice edged with disbelief. "Are you... are you locking us in this bitch?"

Banks's expression was unyielding. "For 48 hours, until you come to your senses and realize what these people are bringing us... nobody leaves without my approval."

"And what the fuck are they bringing us?"

"Obedience."

Mason was so angry his heart rocked. "Banks, you can't—"

"Get out," Banks barked, cutting him off.

"I won't leave until—"

Suddenly, the doors swung open, and five men entered the room, their presence a physical wall between Mason and Banks.

"Don't make me hurt you, Mason," Banks warned, his voice calm but heavy with menace. "Because we both know you're due, don't we?"

One of the men reached out, his hand brushing Mason's arm. Mason's response was swift. A sharp, calculated punch to the man's jaw that sent him staggering back. The others surged forward, but Mason raised his hands in surrender.

By T. STYLES

"I'm going, I'm going," he said, stepping back slowly. His eyes locked on Banks. "But this isn't over."

"Indeed."

Zoa was ushered into the living room, her arms gripped tightly by four men walking behind her. A blindfold covered her eyes, heightening her confusion. Their rough handling startled her, leaving a trail of bruised pride and rising anger. She winced at their unrelenting grip, and when the blindfold was yanked away she was enraged.

The brightness of the space stung her eyes, forcing her to blink rapidly.

As her vision cleared, she noticed the men retreating from the room. Her focus shifted, landing on Banks, who sat calmly on the leather couch. The bruises on his face were unusual. Who had struck the great Banks Wales?

And did they live to talk about it?

"Banks, what's going on?" She demanded, her voice trembling. "Why were they so rough with me?" She trailed off, searching his face.

"I thought you weren't coming back." Banks leaned forward slightly, resting his elbows on his knees, his gaze unyielding.

"I thought the same," she said flatly.

"So what changed?"

Zoa felt the sting of his words but pushed on. "Listen, I know things didn't go well with us yesterday, but—"

"Didn't go well?" He interrupted sharply; his tone laced with sarcasm. "You made it clear that you didn't want anything else to do with me."

Zoa's heart sank. She took a hesitant step forward, her voice softening. "Banks, you know it's hard for me to stay away from you. I just want things to be smooth. No more pain, no more drama."

"Then you come to the wrong place. And I know you know that."

"Banks, can we—."

"You made your choice, Zoa. It's over."

"Hold up," she said, clutching her chest as though to steady herself. "You're breaking up with me?"

Banks straightened, his stare unwavering. "I'm tired of playing this game. If you don't want to be in my life, there's no use in me pushing anymore. I don't need trouble from a woman who isn't worthy. What I need is a partner. And you aren't it."

Zoa's mind reeled. "Banks, we have our troubles, but—"

"Shut up, bitch," he said, cutting her off. "Here's how this is going to work. You're going to sit here, take a moment to reflect on what you've lost, and when my men are ready, they'll take you to your car. After that, I don't ever want you to return."

Her lips parted, but the words caught in her throat. "What if I don't?" She finally whispered, defiance flickering in her eyes. "What if I don't leave you alone?"

"You don't have a choice," a new voice interjected. Lorna entered the room, her presence as commanding as ever. The stench that accompanied her heavy.

Zoa recoiled, covering her nose with her hand. "What is that foul odor?"

"It doesn't matter," Lorna said sharply, her tone slicing through the air. "What matters is that you are not welcome here. Do you understand?"

"Can I speak to Aliyah?"

"No you may not."

Zoa's eyes darted back to Banks, searching for any hint of support, but his expression remained impassive.

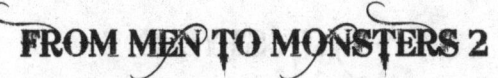

"In a few minutes, my men will return to take you home," Banks said, his tone final. "And like I've told you before, I never want you to call for me to bring you back."

He exited the room, leaving Zoa standing in stunned silence. Her chest tightened as the enormity of his dismissal settled over her.

But she wasn't ready to leave.

Not yet anyway.

Determined to get answers, Zoa turned on her heel, her steps purposeful as she headed toward his office. She had seen him work there countless times, shuffling through papers and documents, rarely locking anything away. Her fingers brushed the cool metal of the doorknob as she approached. If she moved quickly, she might find the answers she needed before his men returned.

Mason, Minnesota, and Walid gathered in Spacey's bedroom. The room was dim, the only light coming from a bedside lamp that cast long shadows across the walls. Spacey sat on the edge of the bed, his back stiff from the

By T. STYLES

earlier injury. He winced slightly as he shifted, but the tension in the room left no time for comfort.

Mason's expression was serious, a folder of documents in his lap. It was time to discuss next steps and the atmosphere crackled with unspoken urgency.

They were just about to dive into the conversation when Spacey rose his hand, sniffing the air. "Hold up," he said, easing himself off the bed. He moved slowly, a hand pressing against his lower back, the other toward the door.

"What's wrong?" Minnesota whispered.

Spacey's eyes narrowed toward the door just as Lorna appeared in the doorway, her hands clasped behind her back. Her presence was as invasive as the sour smell that seemed to follow her everywhere.

"I want to make sure everything is—"

SLAM.

"That's better," he said.

As quickly as she began Spacey ended things by whipping the door in her face.

A sharp banging echoed as Lorna pounded on the door. Annoyed, Spacey opened it again, his expression unapologetic.

"How dare you slam the door on my—"

"You're right," Spacey said, cutting her off.

Then, without missing a beat, he grabbed her hand, moved her closer to the doorway, and slammed the door again. This time, the satisfying sound of it catching her nose with a thud made him grin.

Minnesota and Walid stifled laughter while Mason let out a long, disapproving sigh. "If you knew who she was, you'd know why that was a bad move," Mason said.

"I don't care if she's the devil herself," Spacey replied, settling back on the bed. "Whatever she's gonna do, she'll do it whether I slam the door or not."

"True," Walid said, leaning against the wall, arms crossed.

Mason sat down in the armchair by the window, his hands resting on the arms as he tried to focus the group. "Let's get serious. Banks locked us in for 48 hours. That means in 72 hours, we have to bounce."

"Locked us in. By accident?" Minnesota questioned.

"It wasn't by accident the first time he did it. So now should be no different."

When Spacey gripped his back in pain, Minnesota adjusted Spacey's pillow. "Lie down before you hurt yourself again," she said firmly.

By T. STYLES

Spacey groaned but complied, his movements slow and deliberate. Walid remained against the wall his glare distant as Mason began speaking.

"So were you right? About the church." Walid asked.

"*The Bells Of The Chosen Disciples* is the most dangerous organization I've ever seen for a religious sect," Mason said, his voice low but steady. "When your grandmother passed, and your father was going through his turmoil, Banks always felt responsible. And after his father died, he was convinced it was because of his own sins. He was dope boy rich back then, with more money than he knew what to do with, but he was also searching for answers. They gave him the answers. Told him what to do and how to do it."

Walid nodded grimly. "Sounds like dad. Always looking for something with structure."

"Exactly," Mason continued. "That's how they got him. The church's strict plans, and their rigid rules, resonated with him. And what nobody knows but me, is he used those same rules on this family. Fear. Control. Obedience."

"Like what?" Spacey asked.

"Do you remember when he made a decision to lock everybody down to fly out of the country?"

"I remember. It's when I was dating Arlyndo and didn't want to leave."

"Who is Arlyndo?" Walid asked.

"He was your brother," Mason said.

"It's a long story," Spacey responded, as Walid still had a tough time understanding that although he was siblings with Minnesota, she was not related to Mason.

"Anyway, how he made the decision to lock his family down and get them away, and how he ruled by an iron fist, he learned from them. They had the same philosophy and people died and showed up missing when they disobeyed."

"Was Lorna involved?" Minnesota asked.

"No...she would've been too young. But I don't know about her mother." He sighed and stood up. "The church eventually got into protecting high profile families because they had the manpower, and they were very good at what they did."

"This ain't good at all," Spacey added. "We may be fucked."

"They only had him for 30 or 60 days, but during that time, they made him do more and more crazy shit to see if they had him where they wanted him."

"Like what?" Spacey asked, his voice tinged with unease.

"From eating sand drinks, bugs, living in a cold room for 48 hours with nothing but his underwear, to offering every dime of his wealth," Mason said. "These people had him completely under their control. What's worse is I think he loved it. Being dominated."

"Gross," Spacey said.

"What came next was a bunch of tattoos to replace what he got there. Pain."

Spacey frowned. "You don't think he gave them his money this time do you?"

"I don't know," Mason admitted, his tone heavy with uncertainty. "But I wouldn't be surprised. When I passed their property earlier, they had a brand-new development. It was massive. *The Bells Of The Chosen Disciples* never had a big following, but if they rope in someone like Banks, that's all they need."

Walid shook his head. "So, what's the plan? I'm gonna prepare Aliyah for what's coming and think about ways to get the boys prepared too."

"And I'll talk to Joey," Minnesota said.

Mason sighed and flopped back into the chair. "I'll try to obtain a pulse on Banks. To see how far he's into them for."

"How long are we talking?" Minnesota asked. "Before we move."

"Three days," Mason replied. "I don't see us staying here longer than that."

"Three days it is," Walid said, pushing off the wall.

"Not a day more," Spacey added.

Zoa worked her way through the papers in Banks' desk drawers with a sense of urgency. Her hands trembled slightly as she rifled through the neatly arranged files, careful not to disturb them too much. Her heart pounded in her chest and every so often, her gaze darted to the door, due to the faintest sound outside the room.

Fear pressed down on her, but she forced herself to push forward, even feeling like she only had a few more minutes. Finally Zoa reached for the last drawer and her fingers grazed the smooth edges of its contents until she found an envelope. It bore an address written in bold, precise handwriting.

She got it!

Quickly she pulled out her phone, her hands shaking as she snapped a quick picture. The click of the camera app sounded deafening in the stillness of the room. Next she

sent the photo to Josh with a single tap and immediately called him.

Seconds later, Josh's voice came through. "That's the only thing I found. I believe it's the right address."

"How are you? Are you okay? Because I suggest you get out now while you can."

"I think you're right," Zoa whispered. "Something's going on with Banks. This house feels oppressive and I do believe he's dangerous."

"Just as Aliyah said," Josh replied grimly.

Zoa nodded, even though he couldn't see her. "They're taking me —."

The sound of heavy footsteps filled the hallway and Zoa's stomach sank as five men filed into the office. Their imposing figures blocked the doorway, and behind them, Lorna appeared.

Her presence as overwhelming as the pungent smell that clung to her. "What are you doing in here?" Lorna demanded, her voice cold and sharp.

Zoa hesitated, her mind scrambling for an excuse. "I was just —"

"Stealing."

Zoa didn't have time to protest. Lorna strode across the room with surprising speed, her bony hand snatching the

phone from her grasp. She turned the screen toward herself, her eyes narrowing as she read the name displayed: Josh.

"So you're sleeping with the enemy?" Lorna asked, her tone dripping with suspicion.

In her mind she determined that maybe Banks was right after all. She suddenly felt disloyal for not believing him.

"It's not what you think," Zoa stammered, trying to steady her voice. "I was doing this for —"

"It doesn't matter," Lorna said dismissively, slipping the phone into her pocket. "You're coming with me." She looked back at the men. "Cease her!"

By T. STYLES

CHAPTER FOURTEEN

Walid walked down the dimly lit hallway, his mind churning with thoughts of Lorna and *The Bells Of The Chosen Disciples*. The news had been worse than he could have imagined, and he knew he needed to speak with Aliyah at once. But as he turned the corner, he stopped dead in his tracks.

The corridor was a mess.

Eggs and shattered shells were splattered across the walls and floor, their pungent smell faint but unmistakable. The sticky residue glistened under the overhead lights, causing a chaotic mural of dried yolks and whites. Confused but certain of the culprits, Walid rushed toward the boys' room.

He wasn't gonna hold you, but he was sick of them little niggas.

The door creaked open, and his suspicions were immediately confirmed by the guilty expressions staring back at him. Roman was the first to speak, his voice hurried and apologetic.

"I'm sorry, uncle," he said, his words tumbling out in a rush. "I was just playing. I wanted to see if eggs really break on walls. It was a dumb idea…"

Roman kept talking, his voice a faint hum in Walid's ears as his attention shifted. Because suddenly his gaze landed on Baltimore, his son, standing quietly in the corner. There was something so hauntingly familiar that it sent a shiver down Walid's spine. Memories of his own childhood with his twin brother came flooding back. The mischief, the chaos, and the constant need to clean up after Ace. The weight of those moments pressed down on him, now mirrored in his own son.

Was Baltimore the villain in this new story?

No child should have to feel this kind of stress. Roman, a boy without his mother and father, didn't deserve the burden of guilt his own son was placing on him.

Walid placed a hand on Roman's shoulder, his voice gentle. "No need to apologize, son," he said. "I'll have someone clean it up."

That wasn't good enough for the prince. And so Baltimore's voice cut through the moment in a sharp rude tone. "You're not gonna say anything else to him, father? You're not gonna tell him that he's bad? He hit the walls with eggs! You gotta tell him he's bad!"

Walid straightened, his expression firm but calm. He couldn't believe what he was seeing. "Roman, you come with me and Baltimore you stay here. I'll send Sarah to clean it up."

"Where are you taking him?"

"Don't worry about it."

Without another word, Walid left the room and took Roman into a guestroom. "I know what's happening. I can't talk to you about it now, just know that no one is going to throw you out. You're family. You're my blood."

Roman wrapped his arms around him tightly. It was evident that those were the words he wanted to hear.

"I love you," Roman said.

"I love you too." He kissed him on the head and left the room.

His heart ached as he walked down the hallway. By the time he reached Aliyah's room, the weight of what he needed to say settled heavily between them. "We have to leave within the next 72 hours."

Aliyah's brow furrowed. "Why? What's going on?"

"I just got some information from pops, and I don't trust it here anymore. And I told you when I didn't feel safe here I would let you know."

"Give me more, Walid."

"Father has locked us down for 48 hours. So when the doors open, within 72 hours we will be out."

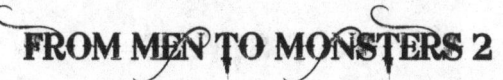

Her eyes searched his face, sensing there was more to his unease. "Whatever you want we will do. But...why do I feel like something else is happening?"

Walid hesitated, his thoughts racing. "There were eggs in the hallway."

She frowned. "I didn't see anything."

"Trust me."

Aliyah shook her head. "Baltimore told me Roman hit the walls with eggs earlier, but when I had someone check, there was nothing there."

"Baby, they are there." He looked at her closely, willing her to understand.

It took a moment, but suddenly, realization dawned on her. "Wait...are you saying Baltimore is doing all of this?" Her voice trembled.

Walid nodded slowly. "My son. Our own son is exhibiting habits of my twin brother."

Aliyah's breath hitched. "I...I don't understand. How?"

"I was so focused on Roman because I was sure he'd follow in Ace's footsteps. I forgot...Ace and I share the same DNA. So if it's possible for him to give birth to a monster, then wouldn't it be the same for me?"

"What's your worse fear?" She asked breathing heavily.

"If my father is snapping…if he is turning for the worse, I need to separate Baltimore from him. I have to break the family curse and do all I can to get him some help."

"So we're going to move away? Like we just talked about."

"I think we may need to move further away than that. Like out the country."

Suddenly, the door burst open. Lorna strode in, her presence commanding and unapologetic.

"There's a family meeting," she announced, her voice sharp. "Come now!"

Bolt sat cross-legged on the plush carpet, his back against the wall, the glow of the television screen illuminating his face. The room was dimly lit, the soft hum of the console blending with the rapid-fire sounds of his video game. His fingers moved quickly over the controller.

The door creaked open, and Bolt barely glanced over his shoulder as Patrick stepped inside, his towering frame casting a shadow across the screen. Bolt's gaze flicked back to the game, unimpressed.

"I thought you were playing with Riot," Patrick said leaning against the doorframe, his arms crossed.

"I was, but he's on the phone now. Probably won't be off for a while."

"Got it."

"What's up though?" Bolt asked, his tone casual as he maneuvered his character through the game.

Patrick's eyes narrowed. "I see you been cozying up to Riot Wales."

Bolt giggled, pausing his game for a brief moment. "Why you call him Riot Wales?"

"That's his name."

"You never say his first and last name together."

Patrick stepped deeper into the room. "I'm saying it now because you getting tight with a Wales won't make you one. You know that, right? You're still gonna be a Louisville."

Bolt sat the controller down on the carpet and turned to face Patrick. "You're a snake. A scared snake at that. Now leave me alone. I'm playing a game."

Patrick stared at him for a moment longer, the room silent except for the faint clicks of the controller. Finally, he nodded and left more enraged than ever.

By T. STYLES

Quinn stepped into Joey's room, her footsteps soft against the polished floor. Joey was already awake, propped slightly on his pillows, his eyes following her as she entered. She placed her bag on the side table and moved to the sink, washing her hands under warm water, the sound of the running faucet filling the quiet room.

"This is different," Joey said, his voice rasping slightly.

Quinn glanced back at him, drying her hands with paper towels. "What do you mean?" She asked, tossing the used towels into the trash.

Joey's brow furrowed as he watched her pull a pair of gloves from the drawer and slide them on. "I can't keep you out of here, and today you come late."

"I'm not late," Quinn replied, her tone even. "I'm on time."

"Got it…" Joey said, chuckling dryly. "I was so used to seeing you around all the time, I forgot you actually have a schedule."

"You mean that you're so busy being mean to me that you didn't care," she shot back, a playful smirk tugging at her lips.

He chuckled again, the sound lighter this time. "So, why the change?"

"It wasn't me," she said simply.

Joey frowned. "Then who was it?"

"The lady. The one who smells badly."

Joey's expression darkened. "Lorna?"

"Yeah,," she confirmed, her voice tinged with frustration. "But it's okay. I don't want to start any trouble."

"Why would Lorna be telling you what time to come in?" He asked, suspicion lacing his tone.

"I told you I need this job, so just leave it alone."

Quinn sighed, pressing the button to adjust Joey's bed so he could sit up straight. She began helping him take off his pajama shirt, her movements gentle yet efficient. "But if you must know she says she's your personal handler," Quinn explained. "And that I don't need to be around as much."

"And you're letting her tell you what to do?"

Quinn giggled lightly. "Don't worry, nobody is gonna stop me from making sure you're good before I leave at the end of my shift."

"All jokes aside," Joey continued, his tone softening slightly, "I'm trying to figure out why she felt it was necessary to tell someone who's helping me what time to come in. It's not like you're bothering me."

Quinn glanced at him, her eyes warm and kind. "So you admit you like having me around," she teased, a playful edge to her voice.

Joey smirked. "I can take you or leave you."

"Hold up," Quinn laughed harder, causing Joey's heart to rock. "You can take or leave me?"

He grinned. "Nah, I'm just fucking with you," he said, his voice softer now. "I really like having you around, Quinn."

"Then here I am."

She walked back to the sink, filling a basin with antiseptic water. The scent of the solution filled the air as she grabbed a warm washcloth and a towel. Returning to Joey's side, she began cleaning his arms and chest with practiced care.

"I want you to know I never mean to pry," Quinn said softly. "It's just that we spend so much time together, and I don't know much about your life."

Joey tilted his head slightly, his voice teasing. "Start by telling me about yours. Do you have a man?"

Quinn laughed lightly. "No. It'd be impossible to do this job with a man."

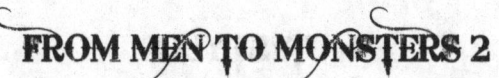

"Why you say that?" Joey asked, raising an eyebrow.

"Because I'm here all day," she replied. "And you are my priority. When would there be time to build a relationship?"

"You can make time for what you want, when you want," Joey said, his tone thoughtful. "Trust me."

"You're right...but I forgot to ask, when I was blindfolded and brought in, I heard steel doors rise and close. Is something going on?"

"Steel doors close." He thought, *are we on lock down?*

Suddenly the door swung open, and Lorna barged in, her presence as jarring as the sour smell that seemed to cling to her. "There's a family meeting. Get him there now. You'll be dismissed shortly after."

"But I want to stay," Quinn responded.

"You can't."

"Listen, I don't appreciate how you fucking talk to her," Joey said. "And I heard what you said about being my handler. But if it's all the same to you, I need you to stay the fuck out my business and the fuck out my way."

Lorna exited quickly.

"What is happening?" She asked, turning back to Joey.

Joey shrugged, his voice laced with dry humor. "Just another day in this Wales family. You just make sure you don't leave my side."

"They couldn't throw me out if they tried."

Josh stood in the stocking room of the library, his hands resting on the edge of the worn oak table. The slight smell of aged books and dust filled the air, a subtle backdrop to his growing frustration. The room was sparsely lit, the overhead light flickering faintly.

The sound of heavy boots pushed toward Josh as Gray Beard and Bald Head entered. Their expressions were serious, their postures rigid.

"What is it, sir?" Gray Beard asked, his voice flat.

Josh exhaled. "I know the address," he said firmly. "We have to go tonight."

Gray Beard exchanged a glance with Bald Head "Are we really talking about this again?"

Josh took a step closer, his voice rising. "I told you what I wanted, and now we've come to that place and time where I need action. Are you going to help me or not?"

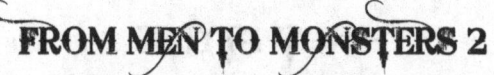

The two men hesitated, their discomfort evident. Bald Head looked away, avoiding Josh's piercing gaze, while Gray Beard folded his arms across his chest.

"We have no problem going after people who owe you," Gray Beard began. "We have no problem fighting for you too, for circumstances that make sense. But this woman said she doesn't want to be bothered."

Josh's jaw tightened, his voice cutting through the room like a blade. "You know what, fuck that shit. Are you standing with me or not?"

Gray Beard's frustration boiled over. "Not," he said, throwing up his hands. "I can't do it. Neither of us. We're not going to support you walking down this path after we told you this family is dangerous. And we're asking you not to go too."

Josh's anger flared, his hands clenching into fists at his sides. It wasn't like they were hearing what she meant to him for the first time, so why the resistance now?

Was there really something to fear?

"You're both fired," he said, the finality of his words hanging in the air. "I'll have your paycheck delivered to you tomorrow. But after that, I never want to see you again."

"If you keep fucking with this family, you may get your wish," Gray Beard said.

CHAPTER FIFTEEN

The tension in the living room was palpable as Banks, Mason, Walid, Minnesota, Spacey, Bolt, Riot, Patrick, Joey, Lorna, and their handlers gathered in a tight circle. Banks sat in a chair looking up at his family. When they heard movement, all eyes turned toward the door as one of the handlers escorted Zoa into the room.

Confused on why she was even there, Mason glanced at Banks, his expression filled with confusion and suspicion. "What's going on, man?"

Banks rose from his seat, his movements deliberate, his gaze sturdy. He took a deep breath before speaking. "I told you all from the onset that we had an enemy, and no one believed me."

"Pops, it's not that no one believed you," Spacey interjected, his voice calm but firm. "It's just the way you were moving—"

"You don't fucking believe me," Banks yelled, cutting him off. His tone was sharp enough to silence the room. "Even though I have proven time after time that I'm right."

"Not much for being humble, I see," Spacey whispered under his breath to Minnesota, earning him a quick jab to the arm.

"Can you please shut the fuck up?" Minnesota said under her breath, her voice tinged with fear. She glanced nervously at their father, terrified that he might overhear.

Banks continued, undeterred. "I was correct about it all because Josh is a threat. In fact, he got my girlfriend involved." He looked over at her and grabbed one of her locs. "I gotta wonder, how long have you been an Opp, beautiful?"

"Banks, please don't do this," Zoa wept softly.

"Did you or did you not agree to help Josh?"

Silence.

"Answer the fucking question!"

"Yes…yes," she said delicately.

A soft gasp rippled through the room as Aliyah, leaning on her cane, entered. Her movements were slow and deliberate, and Walid was instantly by her side, his hand hovering near her back to ensure she didn't stumble.

"I don't understand," Aliyah said softly, her eyes searching Banks' face for clarity. "How does she know Josh?"

Zoa lowered her gaze, her voice barely above a whisper. "He thought you were unsafe," she cried. "He came to me the other day, hoping to confirm that nothing was going on with you. That you were here of your own volition."

Her words hung in the air, heavy with implication. Zoa's eyes moved across the room, lingering briefly on each member of the Wales and Louisville families before settling on Lorna.

She felt like a traitor.

"See...this bitch is and Opp! Just like my last wife."

"You sure know how to pick 'em," Spacey joked.

Minnesota pinched his side.

"Ouch!"

"What makes me mad is that my entire family turned against me. No one believed I was keeping you here for your own good. Now look at—."

"Banks, you are the problem," Zoa continued, "and I'm starting to think that maybe Josh was on to something."

Banks' voice erupted like a thunderclap. "So you think I would actually hurt my family?"

Everybody in the room looked traumatized as fuck.

Including Lorna and now the handlers.

Zoa met his fiery gaze, unflinching. "Look at what you're doing," she said, her voice rising. "Look at how you're treating me! Someone who shared your fucking bed! Rubbed your back." She looked at everyone else. "And look at how you're treating your family! This is not love! It's control and I know you know better."

"Pops, she kinda right," Spacey said. "I mean is it true you locking us in for 48 hours?"

"Father, we can't be in here for that long," Minnesota said. "What if something happens to Aliyah or Joey? I'm talking about an emergency."

"I'm still confused how we got this far away from the goal," Joey said. "Family over everything."

"I'm in control of this bitch!" Banks yelled, his fists clenched at his sides. "And y'all better fall to your knees or die in your graves!"

"Oh my God," Minnesota trembled.

"That's just it...you're not in charge of this family though," Mason shot back. "You crashing the fuck out. And it's a bad look!"

"Nevertheless," Lorna interjected, her voice slicing through the heated exchange. "This person violated all of your trust, and she will be questioned and—."

"We're beyond questioning," Banks said. "She will be dealt with."

"Dealt with?" Minnesota asked, her voice trembling. "What does that mean?"

Lorna looked to Banks for answers. At this point it became clear that the biggest danger in the building was not

By T. STYLES

The Bells Of The Chosen Disciples...but the Bells Of Banks Wales.

Walid stepped forward, his expression resolute. "We not gonna let you touch Zoa father."

Lorna smiled to herself.

Mason stepped up, his voice steady. "He's right. Is that understood?"

"Pops, you not touching her right?" Spacey added.

"She been good to this family," Joey responded.

Banks exhaled deeply, his anger momentarily restrained. "Lorna, please take her away."

She didn't move.

"Now!"

"Cease her," she told the handlers.

Seeing her grabbed, Walid stepped up and was held by two handlers. He fought hard and when the men got rough Banks said, "Stop, Ace. I won't say it again."

"Fuck does that mean?" Walid said breathing heavily.

Zoa's shoulders sagged as Lorna motioned for the handlers to escort her out.

The faint shuffle of their movements and her weeping softly was the only sound as they led her from the room. The door closed with a soft but final click, leaving the family in silence.

Blakeslee sat in the wheelchair, her hands resting loosely on the armrests as Big Debra pushed her down the long, sterile hallway of the *Now and Then Mental Institution*. The squeak of the wheels echoed gently against the cold tile floors.

"I told you, Big Debra, I don't need a wheelchair," Blakeslee said, her voice tinged with agitation.

Big Debra huffed, her grip tightening on the handles. "You walk too slow and too casual for my taste," she replied. "This way, I get you there faster. I got other shit to do."

Blakeslee couldn't help but smirk at being launched down the hallway like a cannonball due to how fast she was pushing. She didn't mind too much, though. It was all part of the odd little adventure her life had become. And to be honest, speaking to a therapist, despite Banks' strict list of forbidden topics, was beginning to help, even if she had to bend the truth with a few name changes here and there.

As they approached her designated room, Blakeslee noticed something odd. Her handler wasn't standing by the door like usual.

"Your handler's not there," Big Debra said, her tone more amused than concerned.

Blakeslee giggled softly, finding the woman's choice of words strangely fitting. How did she know he was a *handler*? "Maybe he had to use the bathroom," she said dryly, brushing off the thought. "I don't know or care."

Big Debra wasn't done. "Hmph. You rich pretty girls always get what you want, huh? Got yourself a man to do everything for you, look after your every need. What about a hard-working big woman like me, huh?"

Blakeslee rolled her eyes and let out a sigh. Without another word, she opened the door and slammed it shut, leaving Big Debra's ass standing on the other side.

Inside, the room was small but comfortable, with soft beige walls and a window that let in just enough light to make it feel less confining.

Blakeslee crossed the room to her phone, which was only turned on four times a day. Since the time was right, she picked it up and began scrolling, her fingers moving quickly over the screen. She was well aware that some of her calls were monitored, a condition of her stay in the facility. But as long as she played by the rules, she was given a little more freedom than most. After all, this wasn't a place that kept her against her will, they told her. She could leave at any time, provided she signed an intimidating mound of paperwork first.

For now, though, leaving wasn't worth the stress. She tucked that knowledge away for later, just in case.

Blakeslee dialed her father's number first. The line rang, and rang, but no one answered. She frowned, ending the call and immediately dialed Mason. Again, no response. Her fingers hovered over the screen as she stared at the phone, her frustration mounting.

Why weren't they answering? Mason, the man who had silently promised to protect her since causing her to lose her mind after the pregnancy loss, had already broken his vow.

Now she was even more annoyed.

She set the phone down with a sharp exhale, her thoughts swirling. Her instincts tickled the scary part in her chest, warning her that something wasn't right.

Blakeslee paced the small room, the cold tile beneath her feet grounding her in the moment.

"What the fuck is going on at Sunset Horrors?"

CHAPTER SIXTEEN

anks stood by the edge of his bed, removing his shirt.
He had barely tossed it aside when the door flew
open, slamming against the wall with a loud bang.
Mason charged in, his expression thunderous.

Before Banks could react, Mason shoved him clear
across the room, sending him staggering backward. The
impact left Banks momentarily stunned, but he quickly
regained his footing.

Mason didn't wait.

He swung a right hook, catching Banks off guard,
followed by a swift left. Since he had on rings, it left a catlike
scratch on his cheek. The room filled with the sound of
heavy breathing and the dull thud of fists connecting. They
weren't friends at the moment. They were sworn enemies.

Through the melee, Banks managed to grab Mason's
arm, shoving him back. Both men paused, chests heaving,
glaring at each other. The air between them was electric,
thick with unspoken tension.

"Are you done?" Banks spat out a plop of blood. He ran
his tongue across the inside of his mouth, tasting more but
ignoring it.

"What the hell is wrong with you?" Mason yelled. His voice reverberated off the walls. "You said Josh was the enemy, and yet you're treating your own people like we're the problem! And Zoa too! I won't let you hurt her!"

Banks straightened, his gaze unwavering. "We go through this every four or five years," he said, his tone measured but laced with frustration. "I warn you about a threat, and every time, all of you act like it's a joke. Like it's some kind of game. But every damn time, I'm right. Even when it came to her. After all, a bitch will be a bitch. Why should we care?"

"You 'bout to do something you won't be able to come back from."

He stepped closer, his voice rising. "That woman was working with Josh! She was in my office, Mason. And yet everyone's acting like I'm the villain."

"Because you treat us like property!" Mason shot back, his eyes blazing. "These are grown adults you talking about! The only exceptions are Sugar, Roman, and Baltimore. Don't you get it? This doesn't fly anymore."

Banks shook his head dismissively. "Nobody cares about this family more than me."

"Are we able to leave or not?" Mason asked, his patience wearing thin.

  By T. STYLES

Banks sat on the edge of the bed, his back to Mason. He stayed silent for a moment, his shoulders tense.

"Banks," Mason pressed, his voice sharp. "Are we able to leave or are we your prisoners?"

Banks finally turned, his expression unreadable. "I told you 48 hours...so wait until then."

Mason's jaw clenched. "Your arrogance will be your undoing."

Banks stood, pacing the room. "You know, I hear people praying to some so-called protector in the sky. But the real protectors. They're men like me. Men willing to do the hard things no one else will."

"Stop it," Mason said, pointing a finger at him. "This isn't about handlers or safety, and you know it. This is about control. You lost it when Ace died, and now you're terrified of losing it again."

Mason stepped closer, his voice low but forceful. "Open the doors and let us leave."

"I just told you no," Banks growled.

Mason smirked bitterly. "Do you think I'll let you keep us here? This house, the casket you built for us is the one you'll bury yourself in." Mason stormed out.

Josh pulled his sleek Mercedes into the circular driveway of the large home. The gravel crunched beneath the tires as he slowed to a stop. For a moment, he remained seated, gripping the wheel tightly. Though the night was dark, the golden glow of lights inside the house illuminated figures moving back and forth behind the curtains.

He took a deep breath, the cool leather of the steering wheel firm beneath his fingers and stepped out of the car.

The faint chill of the evening brushed against his face as he walked toward the door. He rang the bell and stood there, waiting. Each second stretched out painfully, his heart pounding loudly in his chest, the sound echoing in his ears. He didn't know which thought made him more nervous.

The possibility of coming face to face with the man he feared most or encountering Walid, someone he was ready to fight if necessary.

Josh's request was simple: he wanted to hear her say it. Face to face. That she was okay. That the life she claimed she wanted — one without him — was real. But the door opening shattered his expectations.

 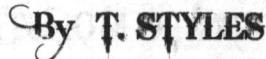

A strikingly beautiful white woman appeared, her strawberry-blonde hair cascading down her back. She wore an apron covered in little strawberry patterns and clutched a cream-colored hand towel, casually wiping her hands. Her smile was bright and warm, yet something about it unsettled him.

"Hello there," she said, her voice cheerful. "How can I help you?"

Josh blinked, momentarily thrown. Over her shoulder, he could see a man lounging on the sofa with a beer in hand, a boy darting back and forth in the living room, and a fluffy white poodle chasing after him. The sight didn't match anything he'd expected.

"Sir?" She prompted, tilting her head slightly. "Is there something I can help you with?"

"I'm looking for the Wales family," Josh said, his voice steady despite his growing unease.

Her expression flickered with confusion, as if he'd just asked the most ridiculous question she'd ever heard in her life. "The Wales family?" She repeated, the corner of her mouth twitching with amusement. "I'm sorry, but I don't know who that is. It's just us Bells living here now."

"Bells?" He echoed.

"Yes, Bells. That's our last name."

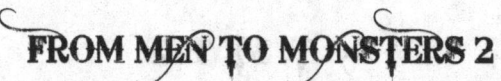

Josh nodded slowly, though doubt crept in. "I must have the wrong house... but are you sure?" His voice hardened slightly, pressing for an answer.

"I'm positive," she said, her smile unwavering.

Yet something in his gut told him she was lying. Despite her beautiful face and welcoming demeanor, there was a coldness to her that he couldn't shake.

He decided to push harder.

"Well can I come in and check?" He asked, the request enough to draw the attention of the man on the sofa. Though far enough away to have missed most of the exchange, the man's posture stiffened noticeably.

The woman's smile faltered, her tone cooling. "I'm sorry, sir. We don't allow strangers into our home. I'm sure you can understand."

Josh exhaled, his patience ending. "Then I'll leave and come back with the police. If there's nothing going on, I'm sure it'll be quick. But if there is..."

Her smile vanished entirely. In an instant, her once radiant features twisted into something grotesque. Wrinkles appeared on her forehead, deepening as her eyes darkened into two soulless voids. The warmth she exuded earlier evaporated, leaving behind an icy menace.

By T. STYLES

"Get off my porch," she said, her voice devoid of the cheer it held just moments ago.

Josh hesitated for a beat before turning to leave. But as he descended the steps, reaching the third, something heavy came down over his head.

A potato sack.

The rough burlap scratched against his skin as he struggled, the world around him spiraling into chaos. A pair of strong hands grabbed him, yanking him backward with a force that stole his breath.

The last sound he heard before being dragged inside was the sharp slam of the door, sealing his fate.

CHAPTER SEVENTEEN

Lorna stepped out of the bathroom, the steam billowing behind her, warm and thick. A white towel was wrapped snugly around her body, her skin still damp but clean and, for once, free of the odor that had trailed her for as long as anyone in Sunset Haven could remember. She moved to the mirror, combing her long hair back into a tight bun atop her head. Her sharp eyes scanned her reflection, and a rare smirk touched her lips.

"Not too bad," she murmured to herself.

After slipping into a pair of black tights and an oversized black sweatshirt, she slid her feet into red fluffy flip-flops. The plush material felt oddly comforting against her toes. With her ritual nearly complete, she headed toward the kitchen for her tea. Her steps echoing faintly down the grand hallways, and past whispers within the mansion.

Once in the kitchen, the smell of freshly brewed chamomile filled the air as she poured the steaming liquid into her cup, the warmth spreading through her fingers as she cradled it. With her tea in hand, she made her way to one of the smaller, rarely used rooms in the mansion. It was sparsely decorated.

By T. STYLES

A couch, a single chair, and a small table, but she liked it for its solitude. It was her space to think, away from the chaos that she helped orchestrate. As she entered, preparing to close the door behind her, Mason appeared in the doorway, his expression dark. She let out an exasperated sigh.

"I don't have time for this," she said, her voice steady as she sipped her tea.

"Well, I guess you going to have to make time then, won't you?" Mason stepped into the room.

She took a slow, deliberate breath, setting her tea down on the table. "What do you want from me?"

Mason's gaze locked onto hers. "I know who you are and what you're about."

Lorna raised an eyebrow, feigning amusement. "And what am I? Who am I? Since you seem to know everything."

"You're a woman who craves power," Mason said bluntly, his tone edged with accusation.

She nodded, her lips curling into a sly smile. "Very perceptive. And very wrong."

"So, what did he offer you? How much? Tell me, and I'll pay it."

Lorna's laughter filled the small room, sharp and mocking. She laughed so hard she had to steady herself

against the table, her tea rippling in its cup. Mason's fists clenched at his sides.

"What's funny?"

"If it's true and I am who you say I am, why would I bother with the ATM when I literally have the bank?"

She took another slow sip of her tea, letting the tension hang in the air for a moment longer before walking out of the room.

After attempting to use the internet to no avail, Mason grabbed his cell phone. He tried again and still the screen read *No Service*. Confused, he headed back into the hallway, and nearly collided with Minnesota, who was pacing with her phone in hand. She looked up, her face etched with frustration.

"My cell doesn't work," she said, holding up the device as if it might suddenly spring to life.

Mason frowned, raising his own phone. "Mine doesn't either."

Before either of them could process the situation further, Spacey appeared at the end of the hallway, his gait uneven. One hand clutched his lower back, while the other waved his phone in the air as though searching for a signal.

"Yo, my cell's not working," Spacey grumbled, his voice tinged with irritation. "It just keeps getting worse and worse."

Mason and Minnesota exchanged uneasy glances, but before they could respond, Walid joined them. His expression was calm but laced with suspicion.

"Let me guess," Walid said, holding up his own phone. "Y'all's phones are out too?"

The four of them stood there in the dimly lit hallway, their breaths mingling with the faint hum of the house's central air system. For a moment, no one said a word. The unspoken realization settled over them like a wet blanket.

This wasn't a coincidence.

Banks had created a home where he was able to block all outside interferences and connections.

"He got a Jammer," Walid said.

"Yep," Mason responded.

Spacey let out a sharp laugh, devoid of humor. "He really out here on his warden shit."

"My family is in here," Walid said plainly. "This not gonna fly with me."

"Me either," Mason said.

The group fell silent again, the weight of their shared predicament pressing down on them. Mason's mind raced as he considered the implications. No calls, no messages, no way to reach anyone beyond the suffocating walls of this house. Banks had taken their last lifeline and severed it without warning.

"We need a plan," Walid said. "A plan he won't see coming."

The group slowly dispersed, each retreating to their own rooms with the oppressive weight of the situation hanging over their heads.

CHAPTER EIGHTEEN
MOMENTS EARLIER

Patrick was a young man, but he was far from mature. After being called a bitch by Bolt, and seeing how Banks was showing strength over everyone, he decided he wanted the same power.

His anger simmered beneath the surface, fueled by Bolt's choice to spend his time with Riot instead of him. Frustrated and restless, Patrick prowled the hallways, searching for something…anything…to distract him from the sting of rejection. Mischief seemed like the perfect solution.

At the end of the hallway, he spotted his grandfather deep in conversation with Minnesota, Walid, and Spacey. Their low voices and occasional nods conveyed an air of importance, but Patrick had no interest in their discussion. Instead, he turned down another corridor, his mind set on exploring Mason's room.

He knew his grandfather wasn't keen on uninvited visitors, but Patrick was too restless to care. He wanted something to disrupt the monotony, to spark even the smallest thrill. To show who he could be.

So as he slipped into Mason's room, closing the door softly behind him, he knew exactly what he was looking for. The room was orderly, everything in its place, as though Mason's personality extended to even the smallest details.

On the prowl, Patrick moved toward the dresser, his fingers tracing the smooth wood surface before he pulled open the first drawer, his fingertips grazing the neatly folded shirts. One by one, he opened the drawers, treating each like a treasure chest filled with secrets waiting to be uncovered.

Unlike him, nobody tried Mason.

And he liked that about his grandfather.

Drawer after drawer, he rifled through Mason's belongings, looking for that special thing. He was getting frustrated and annoyed that he was coming up short.

But as he turned to leave, something caught his eye. A small box tucked away in the bottom drawer. Intrigued, Patrick knelt down and slid it open. The box was plain, unassuming, but its weight in his hands hinted at something important. With growing curiosity, he lifted the lid and froze.

Inside was a silver .25 handgun.

It was small but lethal, its sleek metal surface glinting under the soft overhead light. Patrick's lips curled into a

  **By T. STYLES**

smile as he picked it up, his finger hovering just above the trigger.

A little too close to be considered safe.

The cold metal felt oddly reassuring in his hand, a sensation he hadn't anticipated. A rush of adrenaline surged through him, feeding his restless energy.

Tucking the gun into the back of his jeans, Patrick stood and slid the drawer shut with deliberate care. For a fleeting moment, the anger and frustration that had been gnawing at him dissipated, replaced by a new sense of control.

As he exited the room, Patrick couldn't help but glance back over his shoulder. The slight thrill of what he possessed lingered in the air.

Walid stormed through the dimly lit corridors of Sunset Haven, his fists clenched at his sides and his jaw set with determination. He had spent the last hour dealing with his son's latest spiral...fires, destruction, chaos...and he was done.

This time, nothing or nobody would stop him from speaking to Banks directly.

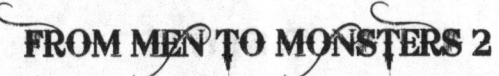

When he reached Banks' door, fully prepared to demand answers and force his father to open the mansion, he noticed it was locked.

There were no handlers, guards or Lorna between him and the man who held all the power. And still he couldn't get inside.

His heart pounded as he pressed his palms flat against the cold surface, his voice breaking the silence.

"Father," Walid called out, his voice raw with a mix of anger and desperation. "Please, just... open the doors. Let Zoa go. You have to stop this before it's too late. I'm begging you."

He paused, his forehead leaning against the door as his voice softened.

"If you don't... I'm afraid I'll hate you forever. I don't want to feel that way, but you're leaving me no choice."

The words hung heavy in the air, unanswered.

"Then forgive me for whatever I do next."

Zoa and Josh stared at one another, their expressions etched with tension. They were confined to a room deep

within Sunset Haven, a place steeped in secrets that only Banks truly understood. The walls seemed to close in on them, yet there was space.

The room itself was empty.

There was no furniture.

Only padded walls which absorbed every sound, muting even the faintest noise or scream. Tiny holes dotted the ceiling in a meticulous pattern, each one an ominous reminder of the unknown. When the air system kicked on, a cool draft filtered through the vents, causing goosebumps to rise on Zoa's arms.

She couldn't believe the man Banks had turned out to be.

How could she have gotten it so wrong?

Josh paced back and forth, his shoes scuffing lightly against the floor. "We have to think. This can't be the end."

Zoa sat against one wall, her knees pulled to her chest. Her eyes followed Josh as he moved, her voice soft but trembling. "Do you think he's watching us now?"

Josh stopped in his tracks, his head tilting slightly as he scanned the walls and ceiling. "Probably," he said bitterly. "This whole house is one giant surveillance system."

The thought sent a shiver down Zoa's spine. She leaned her head back against the wall, closing her eyes briefly as she tried to steady her breathing.

Seeing her fear, Josh crouched down in front of her, his voice firm but quieter now. "We're going to get out of here," he said, his eyes locking onto hers. "I don't know how yet, but we will."

Zoa opened her eyes. "You keep saying that," she whispered. "But what if we don't? What if this is it for us?"

Josh clenched his jaw, his hands curling into fists at his sides. "It's not. I won't let it be."

They fell into a heavy silence as Zoa saw something puzzling. She glanced up at the ceiling again, her gaze lingering on the tiny dark holes. "What do you think those are for?"

Josh followed her line of sight, his brow furrowing. "Ventilation," he said after a moment. "At least, that's what it looks like."

"Or something worse."

He eased next to her and placed his right arm around her shoulder, pulling her in closely. The room fell silent again, save for the faint hum of the air system.

"Am I wrong for being happy that you're here?" She said. "That I don't have to be alone."

"You're human. So no. And if this is the end, I'm glad I'm here with you too."

Banks sat in his lounge, a tumbler of whiskey in his hand. The amber liquid caught the low light of the room, reflecting softly on the dark leather of his chair.

When he heard a soft knock he looked at the camera outside the closed lounge. This time it wasn't a family member. It was someone different and he was intrigued. He pressed a button, and the quiet click of the door filled the space, allowing her entry.

Aliyah stepped in, leaning on a cane for support. Her movements were deliberate, her face calm but lined with the weight of unspoken thoughts. She made her way to the recliner across from him and lowered herself into it with quiet grace.

Despite her injuries, she exuded a quiet resilience that caught Banks' attention. He studied her for a moment, then spoke. "Thanks for meeting with me."

"Where is my son?"

"With Baltimore."

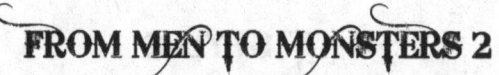

Banks nodded. "Despite everything that's happened to you, you're still beautiful," he said, his voice steady. "And I know how hard that can be."

Aliyah tilted her head, confused. "I don't understand."

He leaned forward slightly, swirling the whiskey in his glass. "I know how difficult it is to keep up appearances," he said, his tone softer now. "To look composed when you feel anything but."

She nodded slowly, understanding his meaning. "Is Josh here?" She asked, her voice calm but tinged with urgency.

Banks raised an eyebrow, a faint smile playing on his lips. "Yes."

Her heart dropped. "Can you at least let me see him?"

He leaned back in his chair, the leather creaking softly. "You love him, don't you?"

"That's not the case," Aliyah said quickly, her gaze unwavering.

"Then tell me something. I mean convince me why I should give you what you're asking."

Aliyah hesitated, then met his eyes. "When I was going through…a moment with your son, he was the one I turned to for comfort. And I don't think he would do anything to

By T. STYLES

hurt this family, so I don't believe he's on the enemy's list. Instead, I believe you used him as an excuse."

"And why would I do that?"

"For not loving you. For not forgetting Ace."

Banks' jaw tightened, and though Aliyah couldn't see it, the vein at his temple began to throb. His grip on the glass tightened as anger simmered beneath his calm exterior. "So, you thought it was smart to come in here and tell me about my life? To take up for another man."

"That's not what I'm doing," Aliyah said quickly, her voice steady but defensive.

"Then what exactly are you doing?" Banks demanded, leaning forward, his gaze piercing.

She took a deep breath. "I mean that if he's here…because it's obvious he's on the list…I want you to let him go. His only crime was making sure I was okay. Because we made a promise," Then she corrected herself. "I made a promise. That if Walid and I ever got together, I would look Josh in the eye and tell him that Walid is who I want."

"Still not impressed."

She paused, her voice quieter now. "I didn't get the chance to do that because I was hurt. I thought a phone call would be enough. But it's not." Her eyes met his,

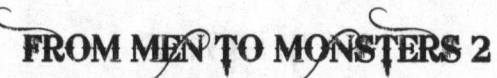

FROM MEN TO MONSTERS 2   191

unwavering. "And I'm asking you…please don't blame him for worrying about me."

Banks sat silently for a moment, his gaze hard and unreadable. Finally, he spoke. "You are a member of the Wales family."

"I am," Aliyah said, without hesitation. She saw no issue with his words.

"And for us, outsiders are trouble. So seeing him won't do the good you think it will. It would only make matters more complicated." Banks drained the last of his whiskey and set the glass down with a deliberate motion. "Go take care of yourself, Aliyah. I've got it from here."

anks and Lorna sat in the control room, a space humming with quiet efficiency. The room was the heart of Sunset Haven, containing every system necessary to keep the house running smoothly. Monitors flickered with various views of the estate, their cold glow casting ghostly reflections on the steel walls. The air was cool and dry, tinged with the faint metallic scent of electronics.

A single key, attached to a beautiful gold bracelet, hung from Banks' wrist. It was the only key to the room, a symbol of his absolute control. For a moment, he sat motionless in front of the central monitor, his piercing gaze fixed on the screen that displayed Josh and Zoa in the padded room.

Lorna sat nearby, her hands resting lightly on her lap. She stole occasional glances at Banks, the tension in her posture betraying her inner turmoil. She wanted to say things to him, things to change his mind. Things to address the unspoken question hanging in the air, but she hesitated. Banks, ever perceptive, broke the silence anyway.

"I trust you with my progress because you've never lied to me," he said, his voice low and measured.

"And I won't lie to you now, master," Lorna replied, her tone soft but steady.

"Then what's on your heart?" He questioned, his eyes never leaving the monitor.

Lorna looked down, gathering her thoughts before meeting his gaze. "Do you know why I choose not to bathe so frequently?"

He smiled faintly, the expression devoid of humor. "You choose not to bathe to keep men away," he said. "To keep them off of you. Because despite your beauty, you feel as though your appearance makes you a possession, something to be used, controlled, or put into a box. But by not bathing, you feel as though you retain the power necessary to stay safe."

She nodded slowly. "But it never works," she whispered.

"I know. Men are creatures of habit. They see what they want."

They turned their attention back to the monitor. On the screen, Zoa and Josh were now sitting on the floor, holding each other. Zoa's face was pressed against Josh's chest, her eyes closed as if finding solace in his embrace. The sight stirred something dark within Banks.

"He's only comforting her because they're suffering the same fate," Lorna said quietly. "It's nothing more." She sighed deeply. "May I ask what that fate is?"

"Wait and see."

"But I must know now."

Banks' eyes narrowed, his anger simmering just beneath the surface. "So you're taking their side?"

"Master, I have done everything you've asked," Lorna said, her voice firm but calm. "I've brought my people in from *The Bells Of The Chosen Disciples*. I am conducting order and following the rules you set for us. But this...this is wrong."

Banks stood abruptly, his chair scraping against the floor. He grabbed Lorna's arm, pulling her to her feet with a force that made her wince. "So you're telling me I have a weak person in charge of my progress?" He demanded, his voice cold and cutting. "A weak person who I make my confessions to."

Lorna met his gaze, unflinching. "If you consider me weak because I'm telling you that what you're about to do goes against the guidelines you and I discussed, then that's a problem with you, master, not with me."

For a moment, Banks' anger burned white-hot. He released her arm and turned back to the control panel. He

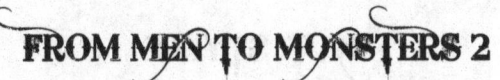

was done speaking to her. It wouldn't change shit anyway. His movements were deliberate, his hand hovering over a series of buttons. With one press, a light mist began to descend over Josh and Zoa in the room.

At first, they looked up, confused.

Then the coughing started.

Soft at first, but quickly escalating into violent fits.

The sound of their hacking breaths reached the control room through the speakers. White foam began to collect at the corners of their mouths as they clung to each other, their bodies shaking with each labored gasp.

Banks' rage deepened as he watched. Their desperate embrace felt like a mockery, a reminder of something he couldn't bear to confront. The sight of their unity in the face of death made him feel small, insignificant. The realization sent him spiraling deeper into his own dark psychosis.

When their coughing ceased, and the room fell silent once more, Banks turned to Lorna. His voice was low and venomous. "Never go against me again, bitch."

"What happens if I do?"

He laughed. "They say money is the root of all evil. They're wrong. Money is the seed. And I have plenty."

Lorna sank into her chair, her composure breaking as tears slid down her face. She wept softly, the sound barely

  By T. STYLES

audible over the hum of the monitors, but the weight of her despair filled the room like a heavy fog.

Two people, who were unaware of their participation in Banks' games were dead.

Blakeslee slipped into a pair of sweatpants and an oversized sweatshirt, the soft fabric brushing against her skin as she moved. Her frustration bubbled beneath the surface, a feeling she couldn't shake. Something was wrong at Sunset Haven.

She could feel it in her bones.

She walked to the door, her bare feet silent against the cold floor. Pulling it open slightly, she glanced down the hallway. Big Debra was nowhere in sight. Blakeslee's heart raced as she weighed her options. Without a second thought, she decided to make a run for it. But before she could hit it for the exit, a familiar voice stopped her cold.

"Where do you think you're going?" Big Debra's voice came from behind, sharp and commanding.

Blakeslee turned, her shoulders tensing. "I was told I'm not a prisoner," she replied, her voice edged with defiance.

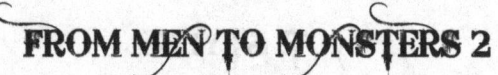

"You're not," Big Debra said, pulling a candy bar from her pocket. She took a large bite, chewing deliberately before continuing. "But that doesn't mean you get to go anywhere you want, either."

"I have to see about my family."

"Then call them," Big Debra shot back, her tone flat.

"They won't answer my calls."

"Then call them again," Big Debra said, shrugging. "You've got five more minutes before the phones are shut off. But trust me, you're not leaving without a proper exit report done in the morning."

"You get on my nerves," Blakeslee let out an exasperated sigh and rolled her eyes. "With your fat ass," she muttered under her breath as she turned and walked back into her room, slamming the door behind her.

The small room felt even more claustrophobic now, the air heavy with her frustration. It was obvious she was getting nowhere with Big Debra. She leaned against the door for a moment, closing her eyes and taking a deep breath. Her options were dwindling, but one thought kept creeping into her mind...a phone call she hadn't considered until now.

The person she was thinking of wasn't someone she trusted entirely. In fact, the only reason she even

By T. STYLES

remembered their number was because of Mason. He left her and this person alone earlier in the year, and the memory lingered like a faint whisper in the back of her mind.

Blakeslee rushed toward the desk, her hands trembling slightly as she picked up the handset. The buttons felt cool under her fingertips as she punched in the number. She hesitated for a brief moment before pressing the final digit, her heart pounding in her chest.

The line rang, and for a second, she thought it might go unanswered. Then, a voice came through, sharp and wary.

"Who's this?"

Blakeslee took a deep breath. "River, it's Blakeslee. I need your help."

River stomped into the mental institution, her Timbs squeaking loudly against the polished floor. Her movements were swift and deliberate, her presence commanding attention. Tall and slender, her tattoo-covered arms and confident stride exuded both toughness and a subtle elegance. Though she leaned into her masculine energy, there was no denying the raw beauty she carried. River was Mason's closest friend outside of Banks, and she was here on a mission.

"Excuse me, ma'am! Where you going?" An employee called out, hurrying after her.

River didn't break her stride. Her eyes scanned the hallway. "I'm looking for Blakeslee Wales!" She yelled, her voice sharp and clear as she began opening and closing doors without hesitation.

"You can't be in here!" Another employee shouted, rushing toward her. The first was soon joined by a second, then a third. Each one barked the same protest, their voices rising in alarm.

But as far as River was concerned they could suck her silicone dick.

River stopped abruptly, her hand moving to her hip where a handgun rested in plain view. She didn't pull it, but the simple act of brushing her fingers against the grip was enough. The commotion quieted as the employees froze in place, their protests dying in their throats. One by one, they backed away, leaving her path clear.

"I'm right here!" Blakeslee's voice called out from further down the hall.

River's head snapped toward the sound, and she strode forward with purpose until she spotted Blakeslee standing in a doorway. "Well, get your stuff and let's bounce!"

Excited, Blakeslee grabbed her belongings and hurried to keep up. As they walked briskly toward the exit, Blakeslee stole a glance at River, a smile spreading across her face.

"You actually came to save me," she said, her voice tinged with gratitude.

River didn't return the smile. Besides, she didn't fuck with the bitch. Instead, her eyes stayed fixed ahead, her expression unreadable. "I didn't come for you," she said flatly. "I came to help Mason."

The two women pushed through the glass doors of the institution and stepped into the crisp evening air. The faint smell of freshly cut grass mingled with the distant hum of traffic. Without a word, they climbed into River's pickup truck, the sound of the doors slamming shut punctuating the end of the ordeal. As the engine roared to life, Blakeslee stole one last glance at the building shrinking in the rearview mirror.

River pulled up to Sunset Haven, her truck engine idling softly in the quiet evening. The imposing estate loomed ahead, its grandeur shrouded in the faint golden glow of its exterior lights. She barely moved from the driver's seat, her hands still gripping the wheel as she looked toward the house.

Eager for answers, Blakeslee stepped out of the car, her heels crunching against the gravel driveway. She paused, turning back toward River. "What you waiting for? Come on, silly."

River shook her head but finally opened the door, stepping out. The two women made their way up to the grand front entrance. As they crossed the threshold into the upper level of the house, Blakeslee immediately noticed something was off. The family members who were supposed to maintain the illusion of normalcy were nowhere to be seen. The silence was heavy, the air filled with a faint, unnatural stillness.

Blakeslee hesitated for a moment before moving toward a corner of the house. She pushed open a discreet door,

 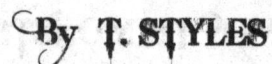

revealing a staircase that descended into the lower levels. They reached another door, and Blakeslee punched in a passcode. The panel blinked green, and the door clicked open.

Knowing her way around, she led River further into the labyrinth of Sunset Haven, her steps quick and purposeful. Finally, they arrived at yet another door, this one heavier, more imposing. Blakeslee entered her code again, but nothing happened.

"What's wrong?" River asked, her voice low but tense. The fact that Mason chose to live in what was perceived as a bomb shelter, fucked her up. "Because this bitch creeping me the fuck out."

Blakeslee frowned, her fingers hovering over the keypad. "I don't know. It won't open."

River crossed her arms. "Maybe they changed the code on you."

"No," Blakeslee said firmly, her voice tinged with frustration. "The code is right. I just—"

Her words were cut off as the door opened with a sharp hiss. Banks stood in the doorway, flanked by three handlers and Lorna. Her eyes flicked between Blakeslee and River, her expression unreadable until she mouthed without Banks knowing, *you should not have come here.*

The first thing he did was snatch all three of River's guns that she hid strategically around her body.

Then he said, "What you doing here?"

He seemed to look through Blakeslee rather than at her. Though their relationship had been strained for a long time, this moment felt different...more distant, more hostile. His expression was that of a man who barely recognized his own child.

"I been trying to get in touch with Mason and Walid," Blakeslee said, her voice faltering slightly under Banks' scrutinizing glare. "I've been calling, but—"

"Why you calling Mason?" Banks interrupted, his tone laced with suspicion. The mention of Walid didn't seem to bother him as much, but the thought of her reaching out to Mason clearly struck a nerve.

Blakeslee hesitated, her mind racing. "Like I said, I was trying to get in touch with—"

"Come with me," Banks commanded, his tone leaving no room for argument.

He turned abruptly, his posture rigid. Blakeslee exchanged a wary glance with River before following him through the now-open door. The handlers and Lorna fell in behind as the air grew colder the further they walked inside.

By T. STYLES

The moment Blakeslee and River crossed the threshold, a loud, mechanical sound echoed through the space. The metallic clanging of heavy doors reverberated around them as thick, steel barriers slammed into place. Blakeslee spun around, her eyes widening in alarm.

"Wait...why did you bring down the steel doors?" She asked, her voice rising.

Banks didn't answer. Instead, he turned his icy gaze back to her. "Come with me. I won't say it again."

Walid, Aliyah, Mason, Spacey, Minnesota, Blakeslee, and River stood in the living room, their unease palpable. Joey and Quinn chose not to come knowing the news would get back to them soon enough.

The air was heavy, thick with anticipation and dread. The faint hum of the house's ventilation system seemed louder as they waited for Banks to speak. Positioned at the center of the room, Banks exuded authority, his handlers flanking him in a protective formation. Lorna stood nearby.

"I started this journey with you all," Banks began, his voice steady but cold, "telling you that we have enemies. There was even a list that myself, Mason, Spacey, and Walid knew about."

"Get to the point," Mason said, tiring of the team meetings.

"Well Josh did come to our home with men. And so I dealt with them."

Aliyah's hand flew to her chest, her breathing shallow. Walid wrapped an arm around her, his grip firm but comforting.

"What does that mean, father?"

"Josh, along with Zoa, were killed earlier. And we all knew how much I cared about that woman. So if I did it, please know that it had to be done."

A collective gasp rippled through the room. The family exchanged wide-eyed glances, their whispered disbeliefs filling the air like static. But it was Mason and Walid who stepped forward, their faces etched with fury.

"Father," Walid began, his voice tight with anger, "As far as we knew, Josh was the issue. But what did Zoa ever do?"

"Exactly," Mason added, his tone sharp. "Once again you out of pocket. The fuck is this shit about!"

 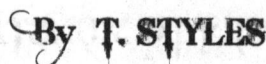

Banks waved a dismissive hand through the air, his expression unreadable. "Per usual, you don't understand me. And I'm tired of explaining myself. So I won't anymore."

Walid's jaw clenched, his voice steady but demanding. "Okay let's do it like this...since you said Josh was the issue and Josh is gone, we free to go right?"

The silence that followed was suffocating. The tension in the room grew heavier with each passing second as the family waited for Banks' response.

Finally, he spoke. "No."

Everyone shook their heads, dragging hands down their faces in frustration. Mason stepped forward, his voice carrying a rare mix of calm and defiance. "At least lets go on the upper level and —."

"We will remain here," he said slowly, deliberately, "until I'm sure there's enough space between our next threat and this moment. I'm done hearing your opinions. Dinner will be served soon. I expect you all to be there."

"We already had dinner," Walid said.

"Uh...well...we'll eat again."

With that, Banks strode out of the room, the handlers following closely behind. The sound of his footsteps faded, leaving the family shaken and uncertain.

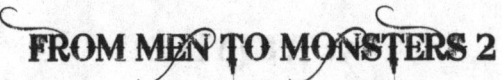

As the group began to disperse, Walid caught sight of Lorna. For a brief moment, her expression softened.

It wasn't in line with Banks' words, and it stopped Walid in his tracks.

He wondered if he had misread her, or if Lorna was someone he could consider an ally. Which they desperately needed right now.

Walid, Mason, Spacey, Blakeslee, River, and Minnesota gathered in Spacey's room. Aliyah had been there earlier, but guilt overwhelmed her. Josh's death weighed heavily on her conscience, and she'd retreated to her own space, seeking solace from her spiraling emotions.

Walid stood near the window, his silhouette outlined by the dim light spilling through the curtains. He took a deep breath before addressing the group. "My father is now the enemy. I've known this for a few days but seeing him like this now...it's different. I honestly believe it's because of Ace. But it doesn't even matter anymore. It's fuck that nigga because we are for self."

His words hung in the air, heavy with implication.

"I'm with you," Spacey said. "Because fuck this shit."

"What I want us to do is brainstorm some ways we can come out of this together. After we do that, we'll lock in a plan and I'll lead it, with all of your help."

"You?" Spacey said. "No offense, but we been dealing with war issues long before you were born."

"You're saying that without remembering what I dealt with in Belize. I know some things too."

"He's right," Mason said. "You head this up, son." He placed a firm hand on his shoulder. "I'm done with old niggas opinions."

Walid sighed. "I truly believe this is our only way out. If we don't do this, I wouldn't be surprised if he hurts us next."

As the group dove into their discussion, they didn't notice Patrick lingering in the hallway just outside the door.

Wanting to play hero, Patrick's hand brushed against the cool metal of the gun tucked into his waistband. Standing there now, listening to the conversation inside, his heart pounded against his ribs.

Maybe he could save the day.

He left in a hurry to find out.

Banks sat in his office, the dim light casting a warm glow over the room. A large glass of whiskey rested in his hand, the amber liquid shimmering as he swirled it absentmindedly. He took a long, deliberate sip before slamming the glass down onto the polished wooden desk, causing splashes of whiskey to scatter across its surface.

Suddenly Patrick appeared in the doorway, hesitant but determined. Banks looked up, his piercing gaze locking onto his.

"Hello, son," Banks said, his tone unusually calm. "You wanna drink with me?" Banks poured liquor down his throat, the sides of his jaw leaving trails like a low energy water fountain.

Patrick froze.

The question caught him off guard. Despite being an adult, Patrick wasn't yet 21, and Banks had never offered to share a drink with him before. So what changed now? The sudden gesture felt strange.

Wrong.

 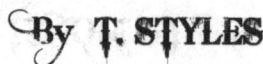

"No, thank you," Patrick replied, his voice steady despite the unease stirring within him.

Banks took another sip, savoring the burn. "Then what do you want?" He asked, his words clipped. "To tell me all the reasons I'm the big bad wolf. Like everyone else."

Patrick swallowed hard, his nerves evident in the slight tremble of his voice. "I want you to let us go."

Banks chuckled, a dry, humorless laugh that filled the room like smoke. "So they sent you in huh?"

"What's that supposed to mean?" Patrick shot back, his voice tinged with defensiveness.

"You're scared," Banks said bluntly, leaning forward in his chair. "You've always been scared. Scared people bully, and I've seen how you treat Riot and everyone else."

Patrick clenched his fists at his sides, his jaw tightening. "So that means you're scared too?" He countered, his tone sharper now. "Since you're bullying everybody else and not letting us leave."

"Son you could walk out the door at any moment and would die an hour later. All you know is money, power and respect."

"You are a bully!" Patrick yelled. If it was true that you hate what you're most like, Patrick was furious.

Banks' expression darkened, his eyes narrowing into a glare. "You don't know shit about me," he growled. "You a weak little nigga, and weak little niggas don't deserve my ear, especially when I'm the one doing all I can to protect you."

"I don't like to be called weak," Patrick said, his voice shaking slightly.

Banks leaned back, his smirk returning. "Then do something about it."

The challenge hung in the air like a heavy cloud. Patrick hesitated for a moment, then reached for the gun tucked into his waistband. His movements were shaky, the weight of the decision pressing heavily on him. Before he could fully raise it, Riot appeared in the doorway behind him, his voice breaking the tense silence.

"Hold up, what the fuck you doing?" Riot demanded, his eyes widening as he took in the scene.

Patrick turned his head sharply toward Riot, the gun trembling in his hand. "I'm stopping him from—."

Riot charged him and the gun went off. The sharp crack of the shot reverberated through the office, leaving a ringing silence in its wake. In the most pain he ever experienced in his life, Patrick let out a scream of agony, collapsing to the floor. Blood began to pour from his leg, staining the carpet beneath him a deep crimson.

Walid and the rest of the group were just finishing their brainstorming session when Riot burst through the doorway. The low murmurs of their conversation ceased immediately as all eyes turned to him. His right hand was slick with blood, and in his left, he held a gun. His face was pale, his breathing uneven.

"Son, what happened?" Spacey demanded, rushing toward him. Suddenly his lower back didn't hurt anymore.

Riot's voice shook as he answered, "It's Patrick. He's been shot."

"Shot?!" Minnesota yelled.

"What the fuck," Blakeslee called out.

"Where is he?" Mason's voice cut through the rising tension, sharp with urgency.

Without waiting for an answer, Mason, Walid, and the others ran toward Banks' office. The distant hum of the house's ventilation system was drowned out by the pounding of their footsteps echoing down the hallway.

When they reached Patrick's body, just outside the heavy door to Banks' office, they found him slumped against the wall. His face was pale, and he let out soft, agonized moans. As he lie wriggling, blood seeped through his jeans, pooling on the floor beneath him.

"Patrick," Mason breathed, crouching down. He assessed the wound quickly, his hands trembling slightly. Then, in a single motion, he scooped Patrick into his arms, grunting under the weight of the grown man.

"Get the medical team," Mason said.

"I sent them away with Sarah the nanny."

"Then open the doors to the mansion, Banks!" Mason bellowed, his voice filled with both fury and desperation. "I need to take my grandson to the hospital!"

Inside the office, Banks sat at his desk, sipping his whiskey. He was busted to the Gods at this point. The warm glow of the desk lamp highlighted the amber liquid in his glass.

"I will do no such thing," Banks replied coldly.

"What you talking about?" Spacey yelled, stepping closer to the door. "You gonna let his grandson possibly die?"

Banks let out a dry chuckle, setting his glass down with a soft clink. "It's a flesh wound," he said dismissively. "He'll survive."

Mason, still holding Patrick, looked at the others in disbelief. His eyes burned with unshed tears as he turned back to the door.

Walid stepped closer. "This is not you, father. You're better than this. I know it."

Banks didn't respond immediately. Instead, he gestured lazily toward the floor inside his office, where the bloody bullet lay, a small but damning piece of evidence. "Like I said it was a flesh wound. The bullet went in and out. He'll be fine. Now get out of my face before things get worse."

The silence that followed was deafening. Mason, Spacey, Walid, River, Blakeslee, Minnesota and the others exchanged glances, their expressions were of shock and seething anger. For a moment, the air was thick with the weight of their collective hatred. It was one thing for Banks to impose his control in the name of protection. It was another to disregard his grandson's life so callously.

Mason turned and began rushing down the hallway, his jaw clenched tightly. The others followed, his steps heavy with unspoken resentment.

"Wait," a voice called softly from behind them. They turned to see Lorna hurrying toward them, her movements uncharacteristically quick. She held a small medical kit in her hands. "Give it to Quinn," Lorna whispered, her voice barely audible. "She's a nurse. Take the boy to her. She'll know what to do."

"Thank you," River said holding the kit for Mason.

"And whatever you do, get that key off of Banks' wrist. It unlocks the control room which unlocks the house."

Mason stared at her for a moment, his expression unreadable. Then he nodded once, before shifting Patrick's weight in his arms and leading the group toward Joey's room.

CHAPTER TWENTY

Walid, Minnesota, Spacey, and Blakeslee entered Walid's office with Riot and Bolt trailing behind them. The room felt cold and unfamiliar, a space Walid rarely used. But now, it seemed like the right place to gather.

Mason was absent, still with Patrick. While Quinn did her best to nurse him back to health, with River remaining at his side.

Joey was in his room in a haze of medication-induced grogginess. The strong dosage of pain medicine left him dazed and struggling to comprehend the chaos unfolding around him.

Meanwhile, Aliyah lay in her room, also so drugged up that Walid doubted she'd wake before the next day. The guilt of Josh's death hung heavily over her, a weight she couldn't shake although Walid wish she'd try.

Walid was about to speak when something caught his eye. He looked up at the corners of his office and noticed small, intricate patterns in the ceiling. Patterns he'd never paid attention to before. He glared and he raised a hand to stop Minnesota just as she opened her mouth to speak. With a firm finger pressed gently across her lips, he motioned for everyone to follow him.

"Come with me," he whispered.

He led them to the bathroom adjacent to the office. The sterile scent of soap and slight traces of mildew greeted them as they stepped inside. Walid's eyes scanned the ceiling carefully and there were no patterns he could see. When he was certain, he closed and locked the door behind them.

"I think our rooms have cameras," he said, his voice low but steady.

"What?" Minnesota whispered sharply, her eyes widening in disbelief. "You don't think father put cameras in our rooms to spy on us, do you? I mean I be naked as fuck in my room. Don't never wear clothes type naked."

"Gross," Spacey said.

Walid's jaw tightened. "I don't trust him right now," he admitted. "At first, I thought this was just about the fact that Ace took his own life...it broke him. But now...now I think it's about something else."

Blakeslee stepped forward, her expression unreadable. "It's about me," she said softly.

Everyone turned to her, their confusion evident.

"What you mean it's about you?" Minnesota asked, her tone cautious.

Blakeslee hesitated for a moment before Spacey broke the silence. "I know exactly what she means."

Spacey leaned against the counter, crossing his arms as he continued. "The meltdown we're seeing in pops. It's not just about Ace. It's about what went down between Mason and Blakeslee too. Those two things happening at the same time. It's the perfect storm."

Walid took a deep breath, his shoulders sagging slightly as realization dawned. "Okay," he began, "this is what we gonna do. From now on, we don't speak in any of the rooms unless it's according to the plan I'm about to lay out. If we stick to it, we might have a chance to get out of here and save ourselves."

"What's the mission of the plan?" Spacey asked.

"If he's going crazy, let's get him there quicker."

CHAPTER TWENTY-ONE

It was three o'clock in the morning, but Banks had still insisted the chefs prepare dinner. The dining room glowed with the warm light of the chandeliers, the soft clinking of silverware and porcelain filling the otherwise heavy silence. Banks sat at the head of the table, his piercing gaze sweeping over Blakeslee, Spacey, Minnesota, Riot, and Bolt. He figured Mason was absent, likely still tending to Patrick...a mere "flesh wound" as he felt.

No matter what, this would be the last dinner Mason missed, Banks said silently. From this point on, he expected loyalty, attendance, obedience. As for River, Banks assumed she was with Mason but she wasn't family so he could care less.

But there was one person who did rub him the wrong way.

"Where's Walid?" Banks asked.

The question hung in the air, heavy and unexpected. Everyone exchanged uncertain glances before Minnesota broke the silence.

"What you mean, where's Walid?" Minnesota said in a low tone.

By T. STYLES

"Yeah, pops, what you talking about?" Spacey added, leaning back in his chair.

"Walid should be here." Banks' expression darkened. "I made it clear that I want everyone here for dinner. So why isn't he?" His tone carried a sharp edge, one that made Riot and Bolt lower their gazes to the table, avoiding eye contact.

Just then, Walid entered the room. The click of his shoes against the polished floor drew everyone's attention. But something about him seemed...off. His movements were too measured, his demeanor too casual, as if he were playing a part rather than simply being himself. His eyes darted around the room briefly before settling on Banks, a faint smirk tugging at his lips.

"Sorry I'm late," Walid said, his tone light, almost dismissive.

Banks nodded slowly, his eyes narrowing as he studied his son. There was something unsettling about the way Walid carried himself. Something wasn't right. "The next time I say be on time for dinner," Banks said, his voice laced with warning, "I expect you to follow it, Walid."

Walid's smirk widened, and he leaned back slightly in his chair. "Since we making announcements can you tell me why you're calling me Walid?"

"Yeah, pops," Spacey interjected, his tone tinged with nervous laughter. "Why you keep calling him Walid?"

"What you talking about?" Banks snapped, his voice rising. "That's Walid."

Minnesota's face paled. "No, father," she said softly. "That's Ace."

Banks' hand gripped the edge of his chair tightly, his knuckles whitening. He had been drinking all day, yes, but he wasn't so far gone as to mistake his own son. His gaze shifted back to Walid...or whoever this was sitting in front of him. The smirk, the demeanor...it was so familiar, yet impossibly wrong.

His thoughts attacked him.

Could he really be losing his mind?

Over the months, the only comfort he'd found after Ace had taken his own life was the knowledge that the "good" twin prevailed. And now, this imposter was seated across from him, mocking his reality.

"Pops," Spacey said gently, his voice trembling. "Walid...Walid took his own life. Don't you remember?"

The room fell into stunned silence. Banks shot to his feet, the motion knocking plates and glasses everywhere. The clatter of silverware against the dishes echoed loudly as his chest heaved with shallow, rapid breaths.

"So y'all lying to me now?" He roared, his voice shaking with fury and something deeper...fear. "Y'all playing mind games?"

The twin across the table, still pretending to be Ace, smirked again, his condescension unmistakable. "Even after all this time, the old man still can't handle his liquor. Walid's weak ass took his own life, pops," he said, his tone mocking. "If you weren't drinking so much, maybe you'd remember that shit."

Banks' breath caught in his throat and as his eyes darted from face to face. None of them met his gaze. His mind scrambled to reconcile what he was hearing with what he thought he knew. At the same time he wasn't there when Ace took his life, so could he be wrong?

"It's not true," he whispered, dragging hands down his face. "This isn't real. This isn't—"

He turned abruptly, storming out of the dining room as the others sat in stunned silence. His footsteps echoed in the hallways, each step harder than the next. The air felt thick, suffocating and his mind raced as he made his way to his office, desperate for answers.

Banks pushed open the heavy door to the confession room, its weight seeming greater than usual. The dim, warm light from a single overhead fixture cast shadows under the chair which was waiting for him.

Lorna was already there, standing in the corner. Her gaze lifted slowly as he entered, her eyes calm yet guarded. Banks closed the door behind him and let out a shaky breath. He moved to the chair in the center and took a seat, his hands trembled slightly as they gripped the armrests.

"I think I'm losing my mind," he said, his voice low, almost a whisper.

Lorna walked closer. She didn't speak, waiting for him to continue.

"My family," he began, his voice cracking. "They're trying to convince me that Walid is gone...and that Ace is here."

The words seemed to hang in the air, heavy and thick. To ease the pressure he massaged his temples but got no relief.

By T. STYLES

"They're lying to me," he said, his voice rising slightly, tinged with desperation. "They have to be. I know my sons." He dropped his hands into his lap and leaned forward, his eyes piercing up into hers. "So I want to ask you, Lorna...which twin survived?"

Lorna inhaled deeply, her expression unreadable for a long moment. Finally, she spoke, her voice calm but firm. "Ace."

Banks placed a hand over his pounding chest as he searched her face for any sign of doubt or deception, but there was none.

"I've always been here to support you," she said quietly, her tone unwavering. "I will continue to help you until this contract is over." Banks nodded slowly, relief and confusion consumed his mind. "But when this is all said and done, I want nothing more to do with you."

Her words were like a slap to the face. Banks' expression shifted from desperation to something colder, harder. "Hold up...you're leaving me too," he said flatly, more a statement than a question.

"I have to," she replied. "The weight of your chaos...it's too much."

"Are you sure?" His question was dark and heavy.

"I am."

Lorna walked to the door, her footsteps echoing softly in the quiet room. She turned back to him, her gaze steady. "Before I leave, did you want to confess?"

"No, you made the only confession I needed to hear."

She nodded and walked out.

He didn't trust her.

He didn't trust any of them for real for real.

So after leaving the confession room, Banks headed toward the control room. He opened the door and was about to enter and then he heard his daughter. Suddenly Minnesota appeared at the end of the hallway, her face pale and stricken with worry. She hurried toward him, "Father, something's wrong with Sugar! You have to come now!"

Banks glared, immediately not trusting her. "What you mean? Did she fall or something?"

"It's her lips," Minnesota stammered, her voice breaking. "They're blue and her breathing sounds funny. You have to come now!"

  By T. STYLES

"Minnie, if you're playing with me, there will be trouble."

"I promise I'm not," she said. "Please come! I'm scared!"

Her concern felt real, her love for the little girl evident in every word. Without more hesitation, Banks followed Minnesota down the hallway. The air seemed to grow heavier with each step.

As Banks disappeared around the corner with Minnesota, Walid and Lorna emerged from the shadows on the opposite end. They moved swiftly but silently, slipping into the open control room. The light hum of the monitors filled the air, their screens flickering with live feeds of Sunset Haven's cameras.

"Let's unlock the doors," Walid said, his voice low but firm. He moved toward the central control panel, his fingers brushing over the keys with purpose. It was difficult because he didn't know what he was looking for. Now that he thought about it, he should've let Spacey do it. "How does it all work?"

"The house is divided into two sides," she said. The right side is nonfunctional without the left. The left literally controls everything which is why the control room is here. And you can lock someone on the right side and it would be nothing they can do. Which is why all of your rooms are on that side, even the kitchen."

"So he has a kitchen on this side too."

"Yes, it's a small one but it's here." Lorna hovered nearby, her sharp eyes scanning the room. "Now be quick," she urged,. "He'll realize nothing's wrong with your little niece in any moment."

Walid tapped buttons rapidly, navigating through the system's layers of security. The screens flashed as he attempted to override the locks, but each attempt was met with a harsh beep and a denial message.

"It's not working," he said to himself, his frustration mounting.

"It needs the key," she said suddenly realizing it. "Damn."

"Are you sure?"

"No. But we need to leave while we still can," Lorna said, glancing nervously at the open doorway. "He could come back at any moment."

Walid shook his head. "Not yet." He turned to another console, his fingers flying across the keyboard. "Show me what he sees," he said. "That part should be easy."

Lorna hesitated for a moment before stepping forward. She pressed a series of buttons, and the screens flickered

again before displaying a grid of live camera feeds. Walid's eyes scanned the images quickly, confirming his suspicion—cameras were active in every room except the bathrooms.

"I knew it," he said quietly, his tone both vindicated and disturbed. The sight of his family being monitored stirred a deep anger within him. "Why did you agree to help me?" He asked.

"What? You're doing this now?"

"I need to know."

"You have kind eyes and I can see your heart."

He wasn't expecting such a poetic statement, but he understood.

"Now hurry up. We have to go now, Walid," Lorna pressed, her voice rising slightly. She tugged at his arm, her unease growing.

"One more thing," he said, his voice steady. He leaned closer to the controls, his hands moving with precision. "I'm not leaving without doing one more thing."

Banks rushed into Sugar's room as Minnesota stood by the bedside, her face pale and etched with worry as Banks scooped Sugar out of her bed and held her into his arms.

Instead of going limp, her small arms wrapped tightly around his neck, clinging to him as if he were her anchor. Banks pulled back slightly, his eyes scanning her face, pausing at her blue-tinged lips. Panic clawed at his chest as he asked, "What's wrong? Sugar, can you breathe?"

She didn't respond.

Just moaned a little.

"Sugar...can you breathe? Are you okay?"

Sugar nodded weakly, her voice soft but steady. "I can now. At first, I was having a hard time but I'm better."

"Well what happened?" Banks demanded, his voice sharp with concern. "What did you eat? Why are your lips blue?"

Sugar looked at Minnesota.

"Sugar, answer me."

"Candy," she replied, her small voice trembling. "I ate some blue candy."

Banks exhaled, his breath shaky with rage. Instead of letting her go, he held her tighter, his hand gently stroking her back. Afterwards he kissed the top of her head before carefully placing her back on the bed. Tucking the blanket around her, he turned to Minnesota glaring.

"I see the games you're playing now." With that he strolled out the room. "You better hope it doesn't come back to bite you."

Banks' thoughts raced as he hurried down the corridor, the cool air brushing against his face. He couldn't shake the unease that had settled in his chest. As he approached the control room, his heart sank.

The door was ajar, but he remembered it was just as he'd left it when he went to see about Sugar.

Stepping inside, he quickly tapped on the keyboards, pulling up the live feeds from the mansion's many cameras. The screens flickered to life, showing various members of his family scattered throughout the house. Everything appeared normal...too normal.

Almost staged.

His fingers flew over the keys as he navigated to the archive footage. But when he attempted to access past

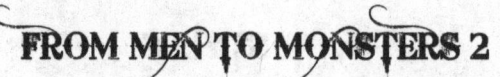

recordings, the screen flashed with an error message: **No Data Available.**

Banks froze, his stomach twisting into a knot. "No," he muttered under his breath, his voice trembling with disbelief. He tried again, the same error appearing. Then again, and again, his frustration growing with each attempt.

Someone had tampered with the system.

His chest tightened as the implications set in.

The footage, his proof, his eyes into the house for the past was gone.

A bead of sweat trickled down his temple as his mind raced through possibilities. Who could have done this? Who dared to undermine his control?

By T. STYLES

CHAPTER TWENTY-TWO

Banks felt like the entire family was conspiring against him so he went to see about it. The weight of their deception gnawed at his mind, and he was determined to uncover the truth. His first stop was Riot. He cornered him in the gym, the air heavy with the scent of sweat and metal. Riot was seated on the bench, his hands gripping a dumbbell, but his gaze didn't waver when Banks asked the question.

"Is Walid alive?" Banks demanded.

Riot locked eyes with him, his expression steady. "Grandfather, that's Ace," he said, his tone firm. "Walid took his own life. Don't you remember?"

Banks narrowed his eyes, searching for any crack in Riot's composure. But if there was hesitation, Riot hid it well.

Banks moved on to Bolt, who stood by the weights, feigning distraction as he adjusted the barbell on the rack. "What about you, Bolt?" Banks pressed. "You're gonna tell me Ace is alive too?"

Bolt hesitated, then glanced briefly at Banks. "It's Ace," he muttered, his hands fumbling slightly with the bar. "Walid's gone." He raised a hand for extra effort. "Honest."

The words felt hollow, and though Bolt's tone was even, Banks couldn't shake the feeling that he was lying.

That everyone was lying.

Everyone was in on the joke but him.

Banks stood in the doorway of Blakeslee's bedroom, framed by the dim light of the hallway as he gazed her way. She was seated on the edge of an armchair, her hands folded tightly in her lap. Banks stepped inside, the weight of his presence filling the room.

"What are you doing here?" He asked sharply, his voice cutting through the silence like a blade.

Blakeslee looked up at him briefly before lowering her gaze again. "I told you. I came to see what's going on with the family," she said quietly. Her voice was steady but tinged with something fragile. After a pause, she glanced up at him again, her eyes searching his face. "Why didn't you believe me?" She asked, her voice trembling slightly. "When you visited me in the hospital months ago after I lost the baby…why didn't you believe me when I said I was pregnant with Mason's child?"

"Because you're a liar. And I don't believe liars."

Blakeslee jumped as though the words had physically struck her. For a moment, her composure faltered, but she quickly regained it, sitting up straighter in her chair. A woman would never lie about a pregnancy, and she hated him for thinking otherwise.

"I'm your flesh and blood, whether you like it or not. And until you do right by me, Banks, things won't ever be right with you…mentally or otherwise."

"Spare me," he said, his voice dripping with disdain. He took a step closer, his eyes narrowing. "Tell me something useful. And if you are honest I won't send you back to that place. Is Walid lying to me?"

Blakeslee hesitated, her shoulders stiffening. She looked down, her fingers fidgeting with the hem of her shirt. When she finally spoke, her voice was barely above a whisper. "I don't know why you keep calling him Walid because he took his life a long time ago."

Joey was next.

Banks found him still groggy in his hospital bed, the room sterile and filled with the faint hum of medical equipment. Joey stirred slightly as Banks leaned in, his face barely illuminated by the soft glow of the bedside monitor.

"What's going on, pops?" Joey mumbled, his voice weak.

"Did you see Walid come in here earlier?"

"Walid?" He moaned. "Pops, Walid's been gone for months. Are you okay?"

Banks straightened, his heart pounding. It was the same answer, yet it gave him no solace. He just didn't believe it was so. He had to go elsewhere for answers.

When Banks approached Aliyah's room, she was lying in the bed in a near-comatose state, her grief over Josh's death rendering her unreachable. Her face was pale, her breathing steady but shallow and it was evident that no answers would come from her either.

There was one place left to go.

Finally, Banks went to Mason. He found him at Patrick's bedside, where the young man lay nursing the self-inflicted gunshot wound. He started to walk away, but his ego wouldn't let him budge as he watched Mason sitting beside Patrick, holding his hand.

Sensing the enemy, Mason didn't even look up as Banks entered the room, leaning against the wall.

"What you want?" Mason asked, his voice low. "To see if he's dead?" He released his grandson's hand.

"You know that's not what I want," Banks replied, his tone measured but tense.

"Then why you in here?"

"So now you hate me?" Banks asked, defensively. "Because your grandson didn't learn how to shoot properly. It's my fault?"

"Don't fuck with me. This ain't a laughing matter," Mason snapped, his voice tight with suppressed rage.

Banks let out a humorless chuckle. "And I don't think it is either."

Mason finally looked up, his eyes hard. "You're right. I fucked Blakeslee."

Banks was stunned, as he wasn't even talking about her. It was obvious that it was coming from a place of rage but it was still true. "Be careful, Mason."

"Nah, it's true. I slept with her. I could tell you she seduced me, or that I needed the attention when I felt alone. But the truth is, she reminded me of you...well of who you used to be. And I let myself do something I never should have."

"Lie to me?"

"Nah, fuck with her mind. She deserved more." He paused. "She caught a stray because of whatever the fuck this was between us."

"Was?"

Neither knew that Blakeslee stood outside the door listening to the whole thing. She certainly didn't expect to hear what Mason said and she felt somewhat better for it too.

"And I'll never forgive myself for that. Because it's my fault she gotta be in that place." He paused. "But make no mistake. You're to blame too."

Banks' anger flared, and before he could stop himself, he stepped forward and struck Mason across the face. The sharp sound of the slap echoed in the room. Mason didn't flinch, didn't move, even as Banks struck him again.

"You done?" Mason asked, his voice calm despite the redness spreading across his cheek. "Because when you are, I've got something else to say too."

Banks remained silent, his chest heaving with anger.

Mason took a deep breath and nodded toward Patrick. "This is a young person," he said, his voice steady. "He may be a man, but he's still young. And you can be mad at me or anyone else in this family, but you never take it out on the youngest. That's not what we do. And you broke code. So you have officially lost me. After its all said and done, I'm done with you. Forever."

By T. STYLES

The words hit harder than any slap. Banks stood frozen, his mind racing as Mason's words sank in. Without his dearest friend, he was nothing. He might as well put a bullet in his head and be done with it all.

Banks turned to leave but paused at the door. "Is Ace alive?" He asked suddenly, throwing Mason off guard.

Mason stared at him, his expression unreadable. "You're selfish. I can't even recognize you anymore."

Before Banks could respond, his eyes landed on the medical kit by Patrick's bedside. He recognized it instantly. It was one of the kits he had ordered, meant for emergencies only. And Lorna had been responsible for distributing them.

The realization hit him like a punch to the gut. Lorna had chosen sides.

This act was unforgivable.

The family was scattered throughout the mansion, each absorbed in their own thoughts when, without warning, the television screens in every room flickered to life. The static

cleared to reveal Lorna sitting in a padded room, her face streaked with tears as she wept silently. Her sobs echoed faintly through the house, carried by the speakers in the system.

"Members of this family," Banks' voice boomed, resonating through the mansion. "This room is where Josh and Zoa took their last breaths. Over the past few days, I made one thing very clear. No one should disobey me. And yet, here we are."

Everyone looked at their screens in horror.

"Lorna picked sides by choosing to be disloyal, and after paying her men, they chose to be disloyal to her. Which is why she's in this situation." He breathed deeply. "But there is more."

The screen shifted abruptly. The sound of a heavy door creaking open filled the air. Suddenly, the image showed Walid being shoved into the same padded room, his expression angry and defiant.

"Everybody in this family knows what Ace put us through," Banks continued, his voice thick with emotion and anger. "And if this is Ace, then it's only fitting that both of them die at the same time."

By T. STYLES

The family erupted into chaos. Cries of protest echoed through the house as each member reacted in disbelief and horror.

"No, dad, don't do this!" Came the desperate shout from Minnesota's room.

Riot's voice cracked with urgency. "Grandfather, stop this, please!"

Even Mason, who had been sitting at Patrick's bedside, bolted upright, startling Patrick from his drug-induced sleep. "No!" Mason yelled, his voice carrying a rare desperation. "Don't do it, Banks!"

Feeling a minute away from fainting, Mason rushed out of the room, his footsteps pounding against the floor as he raced toward the control room. The house seemed alive with panic, the walls reverberating with the echoes of shouts and pleas. It seemed like forever, but finally Mason reached the control room door and began pounding on it with all his might.

"Don't do it!" Mason screamed, his fists slamming against the unyielding metal. His voice cracked as he continued, tears streaming down his face. "Please, don't do this! Please!"

Inside the padded room, Walid stood and did his best to console Lorna. He was done begging his father. If he wanted his blood on his hands so be it. He would just wait for him in the afterlife to get his revenge.

As Mason continued to beat on the door with dear life, Banks' voice reverberated again, louder now, more insistent. "Is that Ace in the room?"

Mason's voice rose to a near wail, raw with emotion. "Don't do it! Don't do it!" He cried. "It's Walid! It's fucking Walid!"

Throughout the house, the family joined the plea's, their voices desperate and full of fear. "It's Walid!" They cried. "It's not Ace! It's Walid!"

For a moment, there was only silence. Then, the door opened, and Walid was removed. But then a strange fog rolled from the ceilings and before they knew it Lorna was coughing and gasping.

Suddenly the screen went black.

His voice still boomed from the speaker.

"Nobody better fuck with me again," he said, his tone chilling in its calmness leaving the house in a heavy silence that felt suffocating. "Haven't I proven to you all what I'm capable of?"

With Walid safe, Mason slumped against the door of the control room, his fists still resting against the cold metal. His breaths came in shallow gasps, the reality of what had just happened sinking in.

In every room, the family members sat motionless, their hearts pounding as the weight of Banks' words settled over them. The mansion felt even more like a prison, its walls closing in, as they realized the true depth of Banks' depravity.

Banks had outplayed them once again.

Or did he?

The living room was steeped in a tense silence. Minnesota, Mason, Spacey, Blakeslee, Riot, Bolt, and River were scattered across the furniture, their faces etched with worry and exhaustion. Then, the door creaked open. All heads turned sharply as Walid stepped inside. Relief flooded the room like a tidal wave, as one by one, they rose to their feet.

Without hesitation, they moved toward him. Mason clasped his son's shoulder, his grip firm and reassuring. Minnesota wrapped her arms around him tightly, tears streaming down her face as the others followed suit. No words were spoken because none were needed.

He was alive.

All was well.

Kinda.

After a moment, he pulled back slightly, his gaze sweeping over each of them before landing on Minnesota. She looked up at him, her expression soft yet confirming.

"We good?"

She nodded slowly.

CHAPTER TWENTY-THREE

Banks woke up in his room, his head throbbing from the alcohol he consumed the night before. The faint scent of whiskey still clung to his skin, mingling with the crispness of freshly laundered sheets. He groaned, pressing his palms against his temples in a vain attempt to dull the ache.

After a moment, he swung his legs over the side of the bed and began getting dressed. He eased into his robe and slippers before heading toward the door. But when he reached for the handle and turned it, it wouldn't budge.

"What's happening?" He said, his voice thick with confusion. He tried again, this time with more force, but the door remained stubbornly shut. His heart began to race as he pushed and pulled, his frustration mounting.

When his gaze fell to his wrist, he froze.

His bracelet was gone.

His mind raced back to the previous day, piecing together fragments of memory. Then it struck him…Sugar.

She had always been able to make the smallest things disappear, but never did he think she would turn this talent on him. A faint smile tugged at his lips as he shook his head, recalling her mischievous antics.

"The blue lips. Well played."

The smile quickly faded as he flopped onto the edge of the bed, the weight of his predicament settling over him.

Minutes later, the door opened, and Walid walked inside. He was calm, his expression serious and unfriendly.

"Father, how are you?" He asked, his voice even.

Banks nodded. "How are you?"

Walid tilted his head slightly, a faint smirk playing on his lips. "Not as good as I'd like to be, considering everything that's going on."

Banks sighed deeply, running a hand through his hair. "So, what's happening?"

Walid's gaze sharpened. "Well," he began, "we've discovered how this house works. And we've decided to allow you access to the right side, while we control the left. This means you will not be able to come and go on your own."

Banks' jaw tightened. "Why?"

"Why?" Walid's smirk disappeared, replaced by a stern expression. "Because you've never truly felt what it's like to be imprisoned. I'm told even when you were on Skull Island, you were in charge of people's lives. Now you'll know what it really feels like to be trapped."

By T. STYLES

Banks leaned forward, his voice rising. "Are you forgetting what happened in Belize? At the hotel. I was locked in there. I know what it's like."

"I haven't forgotten," Walid replied, his tone unwavering. "But even then, you had a plan. You always had a plan. And that plan, as far as I'm concerned, was always about maintaining control over us."

"So what is your plan? Since you think you know everything."

"You will get well, or you won't leave."

"You can't do this," Banks said through clenched teeth.

"I can," Walid countered, his voice steady. "And I will."

Banks' fists clenched, his knuckles whitening. "So how long do you intend to keep this up?"

"We're going to send people in here to help you. They're going to take you back…back to places in your life you don't want to revisit. Maybe then I'll have my father again."

"Anybody who does this is no son of mine."

Walid was crushed but said, "Then so be it."

"I don't need a doctor," Banks snapped. "I don't!"

"You need relief. You need a break."

Banks stood abruptly, his voice trembling with anger. "Don't do this, son."

"You don't have a son remember? Just consider me the head nigga in charge."

With that, Walid turned and left, the door clicking shut behind him.

The silence that followed was deafening. Banks stood motionless for a moment, disbelief etched across his face. Then, rage overtook him. He rushed to the door and began pounding on it with both fists, the sharp, rhythmic sound echoing through the room.

"Bang! Bang! Bang!"

"Walid!" He shouted his voice raw with desperation. "Let me out! This isn't funny!"

No one was laughing.

And no one came.

Slowly, the reality began to sink in. Banks stepped back, his chest heaving, his hands trembling at his sides. He slumped against the door, sliding down to the floor. For the first time in his life, he felt a fear unlike any he'd ever known.

And deep down, he knew — this was only the beginning.

EPILOGUE

The sun dipped low over Sunset Haven, casting its warm, golden glow across the sprawling estate. At the very top of the mansion, Walid sat in the corner of the cozy yet modern living room, surrounded by large windows that framed the serene landscape outside. The air smelled faintly of fresh lavender from the diffuser Aliyah had placed near the window.

Walid leaned forward in his chair, his elbows resting on the edge of a sleek console table as he studied the monitor in front of him. The screen displayed his father, Banks, seated in a starkly lit room in the *down below*. Banks had just finished a session with a therapist and now sat at a small table, quietly eating a meal alone. His movements were slow, deliberate, as though each bite weighed heavily on him.

The door behind Walid opened, and Mason stepped inside holding a suitcase. He carried himself with a quiet calm, his presence as steady as ever. Walid glanced up briefly, nodding in acknowledgment before returning his gaze to the screen.

"I don't want you to do it."

Mason sighed. "I have to."

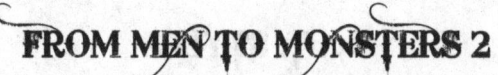

"But what if he hurts you? We still don't know if he's angry, in revenge mode or has Alzheimer's. I mean he's never had to deal with this type shit alone and—"

"I've known this man all of my life. All of your life too. We started this together, and if need be, we will die together."

This wasn't the answer Walid was trying to hear, but it made him love him all the more. Walid rose and Mason hugged him tightly. He let out a long, tired sigh before letting him go.

"He's a narcissist, pop…"

"Let me go. I need you to know that if this is the end, you have to let me go."

"I don't think I can."

"You can and you will. Just do what we talked about. Lead this family into the light. And if I'm right, that I alone can get through to him by going down memory lane, maybe I can bring us both back to this family."

Walid nodded. "I hope so."

"Now go eat." He looked him in the eyes. "I love you, son."

"I love you too, pops."

Mason walked away and Walid pushed a few buttons. A few moments later he watched until Mason appeared into

250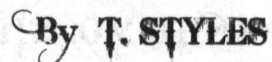

view in the *down below*. Banks got up from his seat slowly and approached him.

A second later, Banks hugged him tightly.

Walid started to cut on the sound but decided to let them have this surprising moment. Being unable to watch much more, he turned the screen off and walked to the table where the rest of the family sat preparing to eat breakfast.

The dining table at the top of Sunset Haven was set. Quinn assisted Joey in his wheelchair making sure to tease him every chance she got, which always seemed to put a smile on his face.

After getting Baltimore and Roman settled, Aliyah sat down, her radiant smile lighting up the room as she helped Sugar adjust her plate. Sugar, cheerful as ever, giggled at something Minnesota had said out of earshot of Walid. With a loaded plate in hand, Minnesota, sat beside her, looking every bit the proud mama, even though she was Sugar's aunt.

Moments later, Spacey sauntered into the room, his usual playful smirk firmly in place as he teased Riot, who had just come from working out with Bolt. Patrick followed close behind, still moving cautiously but showing marked improvement since he was shot and now had to use a cane.

Walid took his seat as everyone settled in, the soft clinking of silverware and low murmurs of conversation filling the room.

For a moment, they all fell silent, each lost in their own thoughts. Though the table was filled with food and laughter, an unspoken question lingered in the air.

What's next for this family?

Walid glanced around the table, his eyes lingering on each face. There was resilience in them, a determination to move forward despite everything they had endured. He caught Aliyah's gaze, and she gave him a small, reassuring smile.

"Where is Blakeslee?" Walid asked finally, breaking the silence.

"You know how she be coming late and shit," Spacey said. "I'm too hungry to wait on her though."

Walid nodded, deciding to let it go. But if he knew his sister he knew she was always up to something.

And she was.

Deep in the down below, Blakeslee sat in the control room listening to Banks and Mason. She had listened to every session Banks had taken in the past two weeks to see who he really was. She didn't know how, but she would get the closure she needed.

No matter what.

She would do it for her.

She would do it for Ace too.

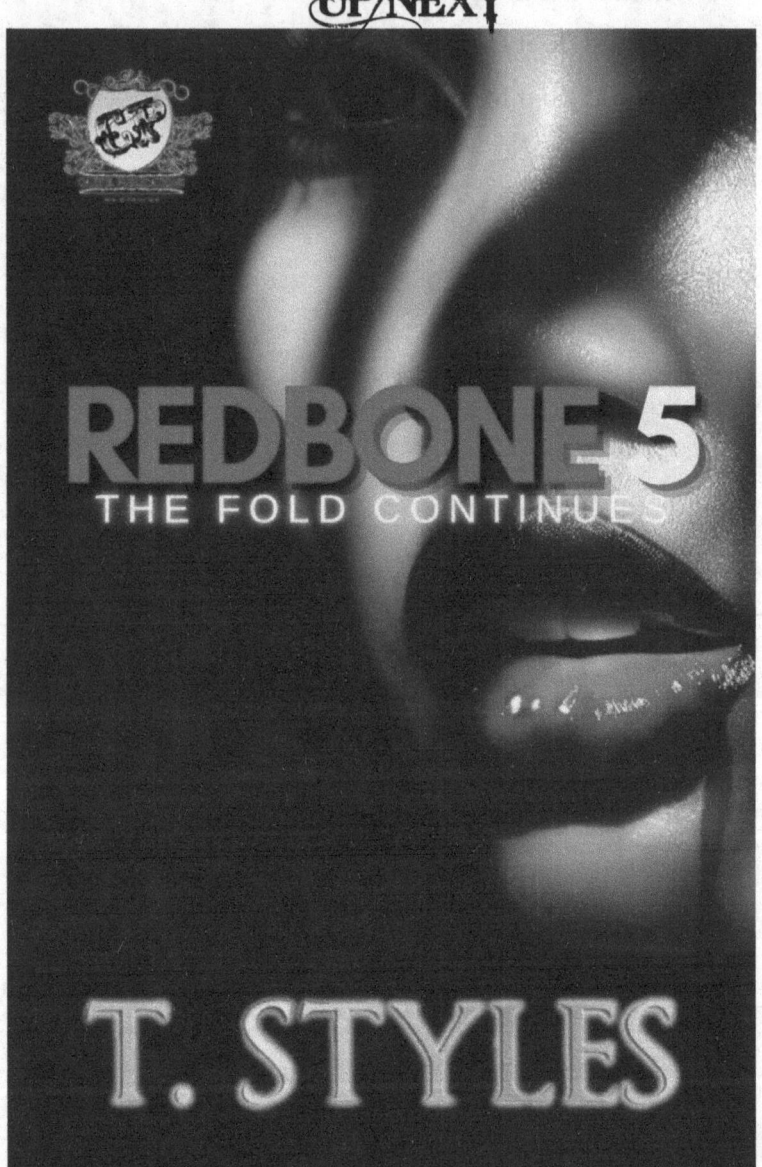

REDBONE 5
THE FOLD CONTINUES

T. STYLES

By T. STYLES

The Cartel Publications Order Form

www.thecartelpublications.com

Inmates **ONLY** receive novels for $14.00 per book **PLUS** shipping fee **PER BOOK.**

(Mail Order **MUST** come from inmate directly to receive discount)

Shyt List 1	$15.00
Shyt List 2	$15.00
Shyt List 3	$15.00
Shyt List 4	$15.00
Shyt List 5	$15.00
Shyt List 6	$15.00
Pitbulls In A Skirt	$15.00
Pitbulls In A Skirt 2	$15.00
Pitbulls In A Skirt 3	$15.00
Pitbulls In A Skirt 4	$15.00
Pitbulls In A Skirt 5	$15.00
Victoria's Secret	$15.00
Poison 1	$15.00
Poison 2	$15.00
Hell Razor Honeys	$15.00
Hell Razor Honeys 2	$15.00
A Hustler's Son	$15.00
A Hustler's Son 2	$15.00
Black and Ugly	$15.00
Black and Ugly As Ever	$15.00
Ms Wayne & The Queens of DC **(LGBTQ+)**	$15.00
Black And The Ugliest	$15.00
Year Of The Crackmom	$15.00
Deadheads	$15.00
The Face That Launched A Thousand Bullets	$15.00
The Unusual Suspects	$15.00
Paid In Blood	$15.00
Raunchy	$15.00
Raunchy 2	$15.00
Raunchy 3	$15.00
Mad Maxxx (4th Book Raunchy Series)	$15.00
Quita's Dayscare Center	$15.00
Quita's Dayscare Center 2	$15.00
Pretty Kings	$15.00
Pretty Kings 2	$15.00
Pretty Kings 3	$15.00
Pretty Kings 4	$15.00

Silence Of The Nine	_____	$15.00
Silence Of The Nine 2	_____	$15.00
Silence Of The Nine 3	_____	$15.00
Prison Throne	_____	$15.00
Drunk & Hot Girls	_____	$15.00
Hersband Material **(LGBTQ+)**	_____	$15.00
The End: How To Write A _____		$15.00
Bestselling Novel In 30 Days (Non-Fiction Guide)		
Upscale Kittens	_____	$15.00
Wake & Bake Boys	_____	$15.00
Young & Dumb	_____	$15.00
Young & Dumb 2: Vyce's Getback _____		$15.00
Tranny 911 **(LGBTQ+)**	_____	$15.00
Tranny 911: Dixie's Rise **(LGBTQ+)** _____		$15.00
First Comes Love, Then Comes Murder _____		$15.00
Luxury Tax	_____	$15.00
The Lying King	_____	$15.00
Crazy Kind Of Love	_____	$15.00
Goon	_____	$15.00
And They Call Me God	_____	$15.00
The Ungrateful Bastards	_____	$15.00
Lipstick Dom **(LGBTQ+)**	_____	$15.00
A School of Dolls **(LGBTQ+))**	_____	$15.00
Hoetic Justice	_____	$15.00
KALI: Raunchy Relived	_____	$15.00
(5th Book in Raunchy Series)		
Skeezers	_____	$15.00
Skeezers 2	_____	$15.00
You Kissed Me, Now I Own You	_____	$15.00
Nefarious	_____	$15.00
Redbone 3: The Rise of The Fold	_____	$15.00
The Fold (4th Redbone Book) _____		$15.00
Clown Niggas	_____	$15.00
The One You Shouldn't Trust _____		$15.00
The WHORE The Wind		
Blew My Way	_____	$15.00
She Brings The Worst Kind	_____	$15.00
The House That Crack Built	_____	$15.00
The House That Crack Built 2 _____		$15.00
The House That Crack Built 3 _____		$15.00
The House That Crack Built 4 _____		$15.00
Level Up **(LGBTQ+)**	_____	$15.00
Villains: It's Savage Season	_____	$15.00
Gay For My Bae **(LGBTQ+)** _____		$15.00
War	_____	$15.00
War 2: All Hell Breaks Loose	_____	$15.00
War 3: The Land Of The Lou's _____		$15.00
War 4: Skull Island	_____	$15.00
War 5: Karma	_____	$15.00
War 6: Envy	_____	$15.00
War 7: Pink Cotton	_____	$15.00
Madjesty vs. Jayden (Novella) _____		$8.99
You Left Me No Choice	_____	$15.00
Truce – A War Saga (War 8)	_____	$15.00
Ask The Streets For Mercy	_____	$15.00
Truce 2 (War 9)	_____	$15.00
An Ace and Walid Very, Very Bad Christmas (War 10) _____		$15.00
Truce 3 – The Sins of The Fathers (War 11) _____		$15.00
Truce 4: The Finale (War 12)	_____	$15.00

By T. STYLES

Treason	_____	$20.00
Treason 2	_____	$20.00
Hersband Material 2 **(LGBTQ+)**	_____	$15.00
The Gods Of Everything Else (War 13)	_____	$15.00
The Gods Of Everything Else 2 (War 14)	_____	$15.00
Treason 3	_____	$15.99
An Ugly Girl's Diary	_____	$15.99
The Gods Of Everything Else 3 (War 15)	_____	$15.99
An Ugly Girl's Diary 2	_____	$19.99
King Dom **(LGBTQ+)**	_____	$19.99
The Gods Of Everything Else 4 (War 16)	_____	$19.99
Raunchy: The Monsters Who Raised Harmony	_____	$19.99
An Ugly Girl's Diary 3	_____	$19.99
From Men To Monsters (War 17)	_____	$19.99
Pretty Kings 5	_____	$19.99
From Men To Monsters 2 (War 18)	_____	$19.99

(**Redbone 1 & 2** are **NOT** Cartel Publications novels and if **ordered** the cost is **FULL** price of $16.00 **each plus shipping. No Exceptions**.)

Please add **$8.00** for shipping and handling fees for up to **(2)**
BOOKS PER ORDER. (INMATES INCLUDED) (See next page for details)

The Cartel Publications * P.O. BOX 486 OWINGS MILLS MD 21117

Name: _____

Address: _____

City/State: _____

Contact/Email: _____

Please allow 10-15 BUSINESS days Before shipping.

***PLEASE NOTE DUE TO **COVID-19** SOME ORDERS MAY TAKE UP TO **3 WEEKS**
OR LONGER
BEFORE THEY SHIP***

The Cartel Publications is *NOT* responsible for *Prison Orders* rejected!

NO RETURNS and NO REFUNDS
NO PERSONAL CHECKS ACCEPTED
STAMPS NO LONGER ACCEPTED

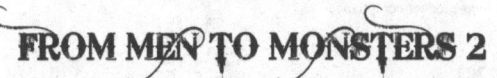